FORESEEN
Beyond Time

Hyper-Dimensional Reality
by
Michael St. Clair

NewMind Technologies

ISBN 978-1-84799-046-4

Order online: http://stores.lulu.com/zensu

*"Build a human being
who can work with the force."*

~ St.Clair

Also by St.Clair

Zen of Stars
Atlantis Oracle

Note

The potentially controversial content of this book by the author of the acclaimed **Zen of Stars** is the result of active remote seeing sessions with time travellers within a quantum hyper-dimensional reality zone. All descriptions and ideas therein may bear resemblance to a developing cosmic potential not known to the dominant paradigm on planet Earth. This paradigm shift is the result of an active imagination. The author is not giving astrological or any other advice. No one ought to feel compelled to take action based on reading **ForeSeen**. The following narrative is a living technology involving a timeless reality of the most advanced kind. The author's imagination will be proven correct. *ForeSeen* is the sequel to *Zen of Stars*.

Contents

Note   4

The Obsidian Mirror   7

1. Surfing The Impossible   17

2. Distant Compassion   27

3. Incoming: *QRC-2137*   31

4. Safe Place Earth   37

5. The Art of Seeing   41

6. Leaving The Maze   45

7. Seers, Prophets & Visionaries   49

8. NewMind Technologies   57

9. The Unseen Conflict   67

10. First Soul Contact   73

11. Invisible Worlds   81

12. Codex From The Future   95

13. The 13th Consciousness   103

14. Guidance Revealed   115

15. The Way Home   121

Astrological Ephemeris 2008-2183   129

St.Clair & The Master of The Light   139

"If one knows how to apply in a three-fold manner this knowing of the mind, all past knowledge lost to memory becomes perfectly clear; and also knowledge of the future thought of as unborn and unconceived."

~ Tibetan Book of The Great Liberation

The Obsidian Mirror

"Mysteries there are in Cosmos that when unveiled fill the world with their light. Let he who would be free from the bonds of darkness first divine the material from the immaterial, the fire from the earth; for he knows that as earth descends to earth, so also fire ascends unto fire and becomes one with fire. He who knows the fire that is within him shall ascend unto the eternal fire and dwell in it eternally."

~ Emerald Tablets of Thoth, The Atlantean

We are living lives devoid of dreams, and yet our dreams are the real and true power behind the world. Humans no longer know how to use their imagination to make the fading shadows of their dreams come true.

In sharing his life time work with you, leading visionary and astrologer Michael St.Clair shares his power to dream. A shared dream empowers the whole tribe of man. The source of our dreams comes from the stars; the power to understand comes from the heart.

As I searched for a way to introduce this work by *The Master of The Light*, I was shown this intense vision: In my quest I turned and looked to the people of the past. I saw a partly sandy beach where the sea had washed up many shells of different shapes and sizes. I knew I could not look within these shells to find the answers that I sought, because as beautiful as the shells were, all of them were empty.

The sea had left the shells upon the shore for people to find; but the real mystery, I was sure, lay within the hidden depths of the waters beyond. I cast my eyes onto the Atlantic Ocean, and there I saw an eagle, its talons reflecting Scorpion energies of rebirth and light. In its talons the eagle held a round obsidian mirror, highly polished, eyes looking through a glass darkly.

Beyond its smoky surface the mirror reflected a light between the worlds: The head of a Jaguar, its green eyes shining brightly, whose teeth became the talons of the eagle held the obsidian mirror in its open mouth.

This was the mystery I was to behold. The Jaguar Serpent became the Rainbow Serpent in its last and final release of energetic power. The dark mirror of obsidian reflected clearly the smoky release of the human soul.

The energies associated with shamanic power are Vortex energies. The upward spiral of the DNA is a pathway of

9

intertwining strands of light filled with a power, which the Mayans long ago knew as the "Rainbow Serpent".

The bright colours of the serpent were reflected within the polished mirrors of obsidian used by the Mayans. The face of the Rainbow Serpent appeared before them in the form of a jaguar. The secret of the jaguar, black as night, held the mystery of the Rainbow Serpent.

The Rainbow Jaguar was the Scorpion doorway to an essential transformation that allowed the apprentice to walk between the worlds. Death was the sign of profound inner enlightenment, and was not something to be feared. Those who could fearlessly cross between the worlds became the peaceful warriors of light who guard our world from the dark lords of the nether world. Those who looked on the surface of the mirror would see their face reflected in the depths and beyond, seeing truth or deeper into inter-dimensional reality.

Scorpio Rising is the power of inner transcendence. Scorpio is ruled by Pluto, the transformer, and Mars, the warrior. For the ancient Egyptians the soaring eagle symbolized the calm but intense and focused energy of Scorpio. Those born with Scorpio rising and planets in the Scorpio sign are determined, intuitive and highly perceptive people; they are natural clairvoyants and can be gifted councillors and healers.

The sacred serpent associated with Scorpio is grounded in earthly reality, but also penetrates into the higher levels of consciousness, thus imparting cosmic wisdom. Transformation is the underlying theme. The serpent sheds outworn habits, beliefs, and illusions, facilitating the death of that which is unnecessary in order to give rise to something useful, functional and new.

St.Clair uses his unique insight into planetary forces to reveal that we are not individuals, as such, but we are representatives of our own destiny, time travellers riding the

10

interplanetary waves of Cosmos. We are souls holding a universal discourse with the stars. The language we use is carried back and forth through background harmonic light frequencies; the same light that forms all that is life.

The findings of our discourse are not always pleasant, as this can become a dialogue of personal misunderstanding and resentment, unless we begin to understand for ourselves why we exist at all, and in doing so take responsibility for our actions bridging the reality of our many lives.

ForeSeen is a reflection of our own selves upon the surface of a highly polished obsidian mirror. If you look further into this dark mirror of the soul there are other worlds beyond this one, whose graduation ceremony is that we understand this world as a perfect reflection of the Spirit.

Each one of us wishes for something better. St.Clair goes beyond wishing – to enact his vision directly here on earth in this most transformative of all times.

From the ancient Sumerians, to Egypt and beyond, palantirs, seeing stones and crystal mirrors have been used throughout the ages for the purpose of divining or seeing and understanding past, present and future. Nostradamus – and who is to say that St.Clair was not in a previous life the doctor from the South of France – used a black obsidian mirror to make the famed predictions.

Many other seers have used obsidian crystal to see the unseen, a practice known to have existed in ancient China as well as in ancient Greece. In Mexico, the Mayan and Aztec god called Tezcatlipoca – *Smoking Mirror* – being a sorcerer, used his mirror to see events unfold, to see into people's hearts and minds, reading thoughts as well as seeing into the future.

Obsidian, a volcanic dark natural glass formed by the cooling of molten lava – a gift from the earth's core – was used by Aztec shamans and magicians for healing what they called *soul loss.* The Aztecs called obsidian "Iztli" or "Teotetl", a divine stone, manifest as earth matter for human divination. Like the Aztecs, some people in parts of Mexico and of South America today still feel that soul loss is a cause of physical illness. The native peoples around the world knew that those who had lost their souls would harm the earth, thus creating a great sickness on the planet.

St.Clair's message is that we have within us an ancient soul awareness, to be activated immediately through our own intent. Many people are here on planet earth to awaken the inner transformative power of the soul. This wake-up call is due in 2013, so predicts the seer St.Clair in this groundbreaking work.

For St.Clair inner transformation is an instant awakening, you only have to apply it. The transformation is about finding our navigator soul, as we come to the end, and in some ways to the most dangerous part of our journey through the harmonic convergence of the worlds.

St.Clair's teaching is that humanity has lost something essential, and if we are to survive as a planetary race we have to re-discover the inner transformative powers of our shared consciousness. Can we know the past – our true history – directly, without the distortions of thought, or are we to stay bound in the linear make believe, falsified descriptions of our ancestry?

The past is the movement of something connected and real, while our fragmented thoughts about the past move away from that connected reality.

If we remain in hiding, running from a deep inner contact with our own planetary soul, we enter into the process of creating the reality St.Clair is warning about – a future of deception and loss of our humanity.

When we inform ourselves and look into the "secrets"

hidden from the mass of human beings living on this planet, St.Clair states that a few of us can command our own destiny, rather than give the control to the other world entities.

Using a natural ability he terms *Psychic Recall*, St.Clair is capable of connecting with the balanced path of his own probable futures. He suggests that coming in from a life time yet to be, those who perceive the negative outcomes can change the future before it happens.

Too often, we carelessly make moves in our lives without paying attention to the consequences. When it is too late to change the outcome, we are left with needless sorrows, regrets and the burden of repair, if repair is even possible. Mankind seems to live continuously in the nebulous past, like victims pushed around by the casual forces of fate. Few realize that we are the drivers of those forces, harvesting the consequences of our own actions.

The ancestors, guiding our future, can warn us of the dangers and urge us to change course before we take the worst possible road to obliteration. It is of vital importance that people on earth rediscover what is a natural time travel ability, and use it to steer mankind away from the rocks and into peaceful waters. The human soul is a time travelling spirit, and physical reality is the ground of being upon which the spirit of the soul journeys through life.

The key to changing our world lies in an essential revolution to take place within the human mind. The "new brain" is activating world-wide. It is a mind beyond thought. The new mind realizes that direct action without thought is based on spirit awareness, the function of direct knowing. The essential spirit is the voyager, and the energy body is the star craft carrying the voyager.

St.Clair warns us that *this* is the major reason why the enemies of mankind are activating a network of pulse electromagnetic interference, attempting thought control. The frequency of these pulsed waves inhibits the brains' ability to see beyond thought, and move beyond fear.

As we approach 2012, and later 2026, with Saturn and Neptune aligned on the cusp of Pisces-Aries, our minds can develop an acute and psychic super awareness, one which St.Clair terms the activation of: *The 13th Consciousness.*

The twelve ages or astrological aeons are different types of awareness that move in cycles of about 26,000 years, out of which the 13th consciousness is the key point of entry, a timelessness through which the knowing from beyond time reaches us. This transformation in consciousness triggers an awareness outside the cycle and a shift towards a new essential revolutionary way of living.

The 13th consciousness knowing is extra-terrestrial by design, in the sense that the teachings come from the stars – via highly advanced carriers of wisdom – who encoded the awareness into a higher light form of intelligence connecting the *Star People Nations.*

The Master of The Light suggests: *"The 13th Consciousness is the Awareness beyond the Web of Life. Only this consciousness can build a human being who can work with the force."*

Earth humans have the inner capacity to be highly evolved beings of light. Designed via our DNA to be time travellers, humans behave as if they are the beggars of this solar system, living without a future, when in reality we are cosmic masters of reality.

In *ForeSeen*, St.Clair's message suggests to the reader that in becoming aware of the danger we instantly take action to avoid it. Seeing is its own action, and intelligent action is without choice. No sane human being would consciously sail a boat onto the rocks. However, you first have to become aware

14

that the rocks are there, as only then can you steer your boat into safety.

This prophetic work by St.Clair is an eloquently formulated and carefully crafted warning to all who read it, that we are coming close to the rocks below the opaque surface of the waters of a falsified history, and that we have to change course to avoid the worst from happening.

Obsidian was used by ancient shamans as a spiritual tool to sharpen their inner and outer vision. St.Clair uses this sharpness to expose the false and to uncover truth. If people do not see through the deception, they may possibly walk into a disaster too terrible to be described in words.

In this sense, *St.Clair is The Obsidian Mirror*. His message to everyone is to live beyond fear. St.Clair's "no fear zone" emanates from within, and its light is essential to bring about necessary change. It is for us to look inside the mirror of the soul and face who we are at every level of our being. When you are afraid you can be controlled, and if you can be controlled, you can be driven onto the rocks of despair, where hidden forces plan to control your future – as well as the future of your children.

Rather than being manipulated by hidden forces, it is time to wake up and take control of your own life, by acting as a sovereign being and not as an ignorant slave of the unseen masters of deception. St.Clair maintains that the divine does exist, and as mankind was born from the divine, is ultimately here to create its own reality – one beyond *control*.

"The Future belongs to him who knows how to wait."
~ Russian Proverb

~ NMT

"When able to attack, we must seem unable; when using our forces, we must seem inactive; when we are near, we must make the enemy believe we are far away; when far away, we must make him believe we are near."

~ Sun Tzu

1
Surfing The Impossible

To overcome doubt and fear is to exist in a state of being set free, and yet it is also the hardest thing for human beings to do. The ending of fear is the only way to use the *invisible light frequencies* encoded within these pages, and to apply the freedom navigations for oneself, inside one's own mind.

Activating the teachings of *The Master of The Light* is to apply the inner guidance of your own higher self, from the future into this moment of your life now and beyond. You become a time traveller as you step into your very own future, and imagine you are guiding yourself from a life yet to be.

*   *   *

The Master of The Light had initiated operation *Dragon Gold* on planet Earth by 11.11.2009, a date he had chosen based on his intricate extra-terrestrial knowing. This was implemented shortly after he and his remote seer team had taken out most paper values floated on the world stock exchanges before the crash. It ended the holdings of all markets and nations.

Dragon Gold – the Nordic Blonds earth project – was neither defined by a fixed purpose, nor was it strictly speaking classified, since its origins did not resonate in the physical world spectrum. Nevertheless it was known, in its effect, to a selected group of connected visionaries.

The technological transfer breakthrough known as *Distant Compassion* transmuted the integration of the extra-terrestrial force outlined in *Zen of Stars*, described as *The Guidance*, was in place by 1999, when Chiron had passed Pluto in line of Antares, the heart of the Scorpion.

This arrangement was not based on a physical transfer of hardware, the breakthrough related to the ability of certain human beings who coordinated the light spectrum resonance creating the art of seeing and the art of foreseeing.

The Guidance and the *Master of The Light* work in a synchronized manner with the mystery of *the force*. The force had formed the *Master of The Light* during a time preceding the descent of earthbound humanity. He was *The 13th Consciousness* of an advanced soul group beginning to interact with mankind. The living technology transmutation was hidden as a sub-reality which most technicians, scientists and spiritually advanced humans lost sight of.

The questions of time lines on earth had been largely misunderstood. Throughout 2009, the confusion about which ET races were the allies of humanity, had become the major disinformation tool in the ongoing struggle to control the human mind. Only few were able to understand which of the ET races was part of the balanced future.

The sub-culture teachings of *The Master of Light,* in his *Codex of The Future,* signalled to mankind that the outer disturbances and the hostile ET force are irrelevant to the development of human populations on earth. Seeing the force within is its own unique action. Humans were being guided to understand the inner phenomenon as the outer forces continued to swirl out of control inside the earth based cycle of events.

Beyond 2020, when Jupiter, Saturn and Pluto had aligned in Capricorn, the structural light frequency of the cosmic management system would command: *"Seeing is its own right action."* The skills of the remote seer brings into being direct action without thought, creating the ability to act in a manner consistent with the Shaolin masters, through the art of not doing. Would the technology masters use this all-encompassing knowing in 2011?

The Master of The Light looked at his red faced, precision made Swiss *SpaceStar* wrist watch – a human touch to his inter-dimensional form. He signalled to me that it was time to move the anti-reality zone back to its original source. We proceeded to enter the time portal in the way he had shown me through our many interactions at *Chillon Castle*.

Approaching November 11th, 2008 we entered the new time zone. He asked me which time shift I wished to study in more depth. I suggested we look into 2027, when the major part of the earth changes had been completed. This was a time when the mass thought pollution had subsided, as a result of the powerful changes in the structure of the earth. By 2027 there was still a peripheral upheaval following the population cleanse, but an intense sense of peace also surrounded the planet at this time.

Information technicians, cooperating with the time lords in fine tuning the sub structure vortices, were convinced that the entities of the dark lords (known also to some earth scientists as the Greys) were attempting to alter the core time lines, and shift mankind back to a thought controlled Matrix based existence.

The entities were apparently moving back into the earth human reality through the 2012 portal, from 40,000 years in the future, while trying to convince mankind that they were physically located in an earth based time zone. The Master of The Light had communicated that we had to pay attention to the complex scam being perpetuated on mankind.

In reality the scam entities had come from planets and star systems they had blown up in previous wars tens of thousands of life times ago, and in order to flee the destruction of their worlds they had shifted to a motionless or timeless zone our ancestors called the *netherworlds*. These entities sought to convince mankind that they physically travel to earth from a physical point in the earth's future. It was an ingenious trick they had played out on mankind over the last 12,000 years.

The *netherworld entities* hide in fragmented zones, where they functioned like clones within hive like structures. Reptilian groups had abducted humans on earth, while attempting to breed a physical sub race. The netherworld deception was known to the original native earth cultures, who had inhabited the earth over thousands of years and whose traces are now all but lost.

Ancient texts and tablets had been left to warn mankind of these netherworld entities. The ancient Egyptian pharaohs, the Toltec mages and Tibetan masters of light had clearly taught their disciples about the true nature of the spiritually disruptive non-human alien presence on earth.

The Nordic Blonds had been working with *The Guidance* from a time line not known to mankind. They had not been able to save the earth, neither via technology nor via spiritual or intellectual teachings. They had tried to achieve certain improvements over millennia, but eventually reassessed their role during the treaty negotiations between Orion, Sirius, Mars, and Earth in 1963. The Nordic Bonds withdrew from Earth, leaving some of their best human assets in place.

The dark lords had, with the help of reptilian sub races, established a complex fabrication of underground time lines and therefore succeeded in the current falsification of human history. They introduced the hostile presence into the earth, and the genetic breeding of human-reptilian clones had been the key factor in dislocating human populations from their own essential destiny. The reptilians created an anti-reality, or cave, in which people were looking at and interacting with the shadow world. This was known to some as *"The Matrix"* – a term which in and of itself can be misleading.

Some anti-reality clones were interacting with society in 1933, wandering among the human populations, devolving by 2001 into diluted fourth or fifth generation collapse. Each following generation was mentally and emotionally more debilitated than its predecessor. The clones distinguish themselves from real humans by their thoughts and actions.

The coherence of the entity breeding programme had begun to deteriorate very rapidly by 2012, and by 2008 the matrix programmers knew that the point the Guidance had warned them about had been reached. The nightmare of the dark lords was manifesting on earth by 2009. The entities were turning on their masters, as the matrix control guidance systems implanted into the entities collapsed.

The Guidance had been warning the dark lords for hundreds of thousands of years, and the experiments eventually backfired as the Kali Yuga came to an end. By 2020 the Guidance had turned the tide on planet earth, bringing in elements with highly advanced genetics to herald the dawn of a new mankind.

The fragmented time lines on earth were the product of the dark lords' entities. The Master of The Light had shown me through the *Chillon Castle* time portal how these things were done, undone, and redone. The intrusion created a slow explosion unfolding over tens of thousands of years. As the *Nordic Blonds* had taught me, one has to have a silent mind to see beyond the illusions of the Matrix.

The Master of The Light maintained that the genetics of the Guidance were the active tools of the *NewMind Consciousness*. Consciousness was generated via genetics, and so his axiomatic tenet was that our team had to configure a human being who is able to work with the force, and hold the frequency of the guidance, which essentially is a light frequency network of cosmic consciousness.

Who and what the Guidance really is and how it works was something The Master of The Light conveyed to me as an unspoken resonance of light. The Guidance is a tool of the primordial ancient life force one could call the Tao, a motionless process in a sea of movement.

This ancient force is the ongoing creation of Cosmos, and the Guidance is its original source intelligence network. The force is essentially silent observation; its existence creates energetic lines, or all the individual incarnations that span across cosmic time and space.

2025 is the Saturn and Neptune alignment, technology and spirituality from the future as one knowing. It was towards, as well as from this time that we worked.

The *Pleiadians* and the *Andromedans* were able, via telepathy, and from their even more advanced position in time space, during the Uranus-Neptune alignment in Aquarius of January 2165, to download to the connected ones the whole techno-spiritual knowing required so that the earth humans could resume their journey and leave planet earth. Bringing mankind to the next level of universal co-existence was to be coordinated by the *Pleiadians*.

One of the key components of knowing, the Master of The Light transferred into my mind, was complex and yet clear: All soul-incarnation lines had to remain spiritually intact. This meant that my life times on other stars and on earth over several thousands of years – in Asia, Egypt and Europe – were *one* stream of consciousness, as I experienced the ending of time. This knowing was defined as the moment when the bridge of time is no longer based on linear thought.

One point of consciousness signified all my incarnations integrated into one life at one moment. When humans do not achieve this inner integration, the woven fabric of the light spirit loses its cohesive resonance. The same cosmic rules applied to the incarnations of the dark lords. This is not easy to perceive at the most basic thought level.

The complete 2012 cosmic timing was something that few could grasp during the night of the soul on planet earth. The timing was a corner stone to understand the *NewMind Technologies* we were in the process of developing.

We operated on the assumption that beyond 2013 we were able to reconfigure an advanced consciousness of humanity, and with it we would achieve the quantum leap for which each one in our network had been working across many millennia and over many incarnations.

The Master of The Light had shown me how a fragmented humanity had essentially destroyed its own future. Human beings in a state of *inner division* had not realized that thought and thinker is one and the same, thus creating the inner fog bank of endless conflict.

Humans who could move without thought, as he did, were operating beyond survival. Who or what had put the fragmented thought virus into the human mind? The Master of Light revealed to me that humans had become a submissive race, controlled via self-centered egoistic thought. Because people on earth agreed to this, the ego had gained strength in the world of man as intelligence had withdrawn.

"Intelligence is defined by the purpose of its use." The Master of The Light brought me back to the time line of the Nordic Blonds – a realm of light where thought no longer existed. Intelligence is faster than thought. The ability to see what is became the energy of silent observation, while the cosmic psyche was able to move through the actions of humans and ETs in unseen ways.

How the star gates operated by the *Tall Whites* would be made operational to the time lords through *The Guidance Network*, was a reality beyond the realm of the earth bound scientists. This was a question beyond spirituality, entering realms of super quantum science, requiring an operational living technology. The Master of The Light defined his existence across the bridge of time expanding his awareness into the earth bound DNA of mankind.

That – in essence – was the dilemma of our seer group: Which future to activate? He saw in my eyes that I had finally understood, we activated the time co-ordinates and opened the inter-stellar vortex into the future. We were moving on now to implement plan B – *NewMind Technologies.*

Using advanced spiritual technology, or techno-spirituality, to create orgone free-energy resonators that bring light and power to the earth is intelligent action. Intelligent action is without choice. The fragmented ego, which is using Reptilian technology to create weapons of mass destruction with the goal to annihilate earth is a lesser use of intelligence, put to a purpose essentially non-human by design.

The Master of The Light mysteriously required each one of us in his team to be self-responsible for his or her own incarnations. He defined the approaching earth transition in these words:

*Intelligence – faster than thought – is defined by the purpose of its use. You focus on the technology of the future, when your minds **are** the technology of the future.*

"The planet was for millions of years one of a category of hundreds that we kept a watch on. It was regarded as having potential because its history had always been one of sudden changes, rapid developments, as rapid degradations, periods of stagnation. Anything could be expected of it..."

~ Doris Lessing, Shikasta

2
Distant Compassion

In his legendary interview with the world's leading TV journalist *Tatjana Yurasova* in Moscow in 2008, The Master of The Light had answered one key question about the issues facing the world, in an unusually cryptic way.

When pressed, he would simply give a few *Tao Te Ch'ing* type references. The ongoing earth changes and tsunamis were a reality akin to the fullness or emptiness of *The Tao*. His key statement at the end of the two hours interview, which had then been aired worldwide, created the number one Google video clip of all time: "Is it true in your opinion that by 2020 over half of the current world population will be dead?"

"If you are asking me this particular question about the future of mankind during the earth changes, it means that you do not understand the dynamics of what is about to happen to this world. Death is an illusion, and the truth of this will become visible to mankind as the earth changes progress."

That is when I knew that he was going operational with *Dragon Gold*. In fact, he told me in 2007 that the code word for the reality team to assemble would be *"death is an illusion."* The connected ones would know how and why, and their understanding of the inner dynamics of the earth changes would define how their counterparts in 2027 configured the new time line into the coming decades.

In November 2008, *The Master of The Light* was holding an informal meeting at *Château Chillon*, inside the grand dining hall. Present around the forty foot long medieval oblong table, standing close to the twenty foot high fireplace, were his information technology specialists, one astrophysicist and a reclusive bio-molecular scientist who knew the secret genetic protocols of the dark lords. A former special intelligence officer from the *European Space Agency* escorted an independent observer from *The Space Federation* into the large hall to oversee the technology transfer. Among the exchanges were

28

aware precious metals. He opened the watch case below the strap and inserted a five millimetre diameter round chip which carried the entire program of *The Space Federation's* information technology unit, plus the new *omni-net* protocol connections with which to download data from one planet to another. The Master of Light preferred to use the more intricate coordinates of the *2013 SpaceStar* watch. Hidden elegantly behind its red face, a mother of pearl screen opened when he pressed the chronograph crown. On the holographic screen he could read the time related alignments on many other planets.

"I prefer my watch," The Master of Light answered, as the envoy readjusted the thin data carrier to interface with the time travel coordinates. The envoy explained how *ESA* and *NASA* were in contact with earth orbiter star crafts and how their extensive traffic had been decoded since 1966, when Uranus aligned with Pluto in Virgo.

During our castle meeting we were informed that The Master of The Light had decided to move from earth with a small group of humans and connected ETs. *NASA* controllers were trying to intercept our team, which amused the participants of our gathering at *Château Chillon,* with silent crafts hovering over the icy Lake of Geneva. An advanced reptilian race was his protection team for the 2137 time location project.

We began moving our network into the 2137 time space, when Pluto in line of fixed star Aldebaran was in opposition to Neptune in line of fixed star Antares. This alignment is a once in a Great Year or 26,000 human years cycle and magnitude one type event. It was from the future time zone that The Master of The Light and his allies operated while interfacing with earth through 2008 to 2013. The meaning of the 2137 alignment was evident to me, since it heralded the moment when time travel came into being as an applied technology, practiced by humans in Cosmos, and shared equally among all civilized cultures interacting with the complex dimensions of outer space, with contact to humanoid species evolving in other star systems.

As to the notion of *NASA* and *Area 51* controllers trying to intercept his projects, the forces protecting mankind over many life times, across the bridge of time, used distant compassion to shield the golden face of reality smiling upon the cosmic mind of man.

Enemies of mankind, counter forces from the past, had become aware of the lower vibration karmic residue blocking their interstellar passage. As part of shifting to a higher level of evolution, these former counter forces had agreed to correct the mistakes of their ancestors around planet earth — returning to protect the seed of mankind, the future protectors of their own species during the end of wars manifestation, the galactic center shift designed through contact with an other dimensional higher race.

The team of high-tech physicists entered the main portal, awaiting the arrival of the first fleet of interstellar shuttles. Ta-Lor accompanied the small group to the first level of departure. They were ready to leave earth.

Ahead of them, at the other end of the light corridor, a large spiral arrow symbol appeared to hover within the smooth aware surface of the door. Ta-Lor raised her hand to match with the rotating center of the spiral arrow. The colours responded, turning from a reddish hue to opaque blue. The energy portal allowed her to enter the installation. One by one, the rest of the team matched their frequencies with the force field of the spiral. The Master of The Light awaited them at the entrance to the quantum field vortex. The team was now ready to interact with *Incoming QRC-2137.*

30

3
Incoming: *"QRC-2137"*

The initial *Quantum Reality Contact – QRC –* emanating from the planet 987 contact back in early September 2001, was initially thought to be a hoax. We handed the contact data over to a tech source and they also thought it was probably a hoax. The participation addresses could not be found in this current time space. Our high tech team suggested the contact could be a secret operation unit testing our security.

In the last report their assessment was simply: *"They definitely have a way to cloak their online presence in a manner that makes it appear to us as if they do not exist. It has to be some kind of a joke; but then again, maybe not."*

Much later our people were able to identify September 2137 as the source of the incoming Quantum Reality Contact. *QRC-2137* had suggested, in their earliest communications with our researchers, that particles never die, they simply shift from one form to the next. We live in a multi-dimensional universe that knows of no death. We, it, everything simply transforms, shifts, rearranges itself. There is no death. Life is eternal. Death is an illusion.

They proposed early on in 2002 that belief systems focusing on death were the ultimate control mechanism of a social system management that seeks to establish its own regime in the middle of an ever transforming eternal cosmic nothingness. The 2137 contact continued its techno-spiritual *teaching* when it began to download into our system what amounted to human frequency survival protocols into and beyond 2165.

It took over six years for the new time travel unit to grow to operational maturity in 2008. We assumed that it was not a computer, or a super-computer we were interfacing with during the contacts. Instead we acted on the fine instinct that we were in touch with an intelligence of a higher realm. Their network taught us how to develop living technologies, and we called their protocols the *NewMind Technologies*.

Ta-Lor, inscrutable, slightly dogmatic, ultra-secretive and extremely disciplined as she was, suggested that we had to take into consideration that we are continually interfacing with computers, as none of us could do this work without them. She insisted that we focus on the information and take *QRC-2137* seriously. Before she left the unit she had begun to work with the *QRC-2137* interface largely alone.

Her breaking rank with the technology unit was a loss for the project, but she was later willing to advise the ESA intelligence experts in Germany who handed the reports and protocols to the Master of The Light. By then we had understood that the advanced technology specialist from ESA was really one of the Nordics assets.

By the end of 2008, within an eleven month period, Ta-Lor had developed integrated interface schemes no one in the science teams thought possible. The new systems were beyond advanced, and clearly not of this earth. This was the key earth contact searchers for extra-terrestrial intelligence had never understood. The inner mechanics of the contact were more important than the outer ones.

My intelligence and research teams suggested we were communicating with an established inner world phenomenon, a hollow earth society, Hyperborean of nature, or present day ET contacts intending to cloak their origins behind some obscure dragon culture. In the initial stages of the project, only Ta-Lor was ready to consider that we were interfacing with our very *own* Quantum Reality.

In response to this each of us began to work with *QRC-2137* within the expertise of our particular fields, be that cosmology, quantum physics, molecular biology, neurology, mathematics and space tech communications. It was an amazingly intricate interface network, known as *Project Dragon Gold*, which was learning to operate with *the guidance*.

Why was the future time interacting with us now?

QRC-2137 told us that we would develop the initial sciences and technology which would later allow them to develop and use the *time travel technology*. We later discovered that behind the technology transfer a very ancient, higher level order of time lords, were guiding the progression of the human species on earth with regard to inter-dimensional space travel.

Across millennia, the Master of The Light had coordinated and overseen essential growth phases in the development of individuals associated with these projects. Time travel technology develops from the spirit's ability to shift time zones without losing its own essential frequencies. This is why the earliest time travellers were located in safe places of advanced high culture.

We began to understand that the human soul is essentially a time traveller, experiencing life in all its stages of growth and form, through interacting directly with time and space. *Project Dragon Gold* was the first step in technology recreating the spirit of the soul. We were being taught how to bring body and the mind into the more advanced quantum-soul field.

Our team began a technology interface with *QRC-2137* at *CERN* near Geneva, a continuation of the Lac Leman time continuum experiments started by the Pleiadians, which lead to the Celtic ancient artefact inter-world exchange. We began to research the tectonic geography of the giant megalithic chalk figure drawn on the landscape at Cerne Abbas, in Dorset, know as the *Cerne Abbas Code*. Our ancestors were highly evolved time travellers.

CERN was to be the European Nuclear Research Centre where the more archaic particle field accelerator was situated. Ahead of schedule, interacting with the crop circle codes, our group redeveloped the lost time travel technology at *La Tène*,

34

Switzerland, where we succeeded in making first contact as we left earth. Our 2137 field experiment, was the year in which the *La Tène Group* – our future – made the technological quantum breakthrough in foreseeing and successfully changing the outcome of our future.

The *QRC-2137* contact did not disclose their point in space-time, from which they were using this technology to make first contact. In 2025, according to our astrophysicists, the technological breakthrough creating the time millennium loop was established, and again in 2047 at a higher level during the Uranus-Pluto millennial opposition alignment, their group refined the technology and began a process of observing.

We presumed that there was also an extra-terrestrial guidance or knowledge exchange within their project, operating at the highest level. By 11.11.2009, the *Pleiadians* and the *Nordics* manifested their treaty on planet earth. *Dragon Gold* was launched.

The project we were working on involved a lot more than just to leave earth. We were able to interact across the bridge of time, using a creative living technology. The *Pleiadians* chose their contacts carefully, interacting with us over many life times, and they seem to have a way to observe and assess our finer energy state. They can observe our individual and collective reactions and we sensed a high level of security concerns in their behaviour.

The La Tène artefact exchange was established to steer us in the direction of making a number of advanced technology breakthroughs that would lead to our planetary development. They began with guiding our bio molecular, medical, cosmological and astrophysical sciences, advancing our own unique understanding of the surrounding molecular events. Understanding the intricate cosmic design behind time travel was essential for those developing the exit strategies.

The Master of The Light had developed the Nordic Blonds *NewMind Technologies* exchange, while activating the 13th consciousness light frequencies within mankind. The defence technology necessary to survive cataclysmic events and time line intrusions by regressive alien civilizations was developed with the assistance of highly advanced protocols. The allies of mankind do not suggest the way ahead, the choice remains ours at all times. Seeing is its own right action.

It was a starry winter night in Moscow. The technicians in the advanced underground studio began the sound check with Siberian TV journalist *Tatjana Yurasova*, his medium of choice. The fact that she was one of our group was not known to the world at large.

The interview created a wave of change in the way people viewed their world, essentially releasing the genie from the dragon bottle. But then, in this incarnation he was willing to take some well calculated risks, because the *Nordic Blonds* knew how to set up the command structure and disguise his presence.

4
Safe Place Earth

"The future belongs to him who knows how to wait."

~ *Russian Proverb*

It was the most covered media event ever – bigger, better and more beautiful than the faked moon landing of Apollo 11. Within an hour most channels worldwide transmitted Tatjana Yurasova's *Safe Place Earth* show live.

The show had by-passed the censorship of the controlled media around the globe – and national governments were left wondering how this feat had been achieved. Within twenty-four hours over four billion people had seen The Master of The Light interview. The broadcast seemed to have been beamed in from some other dimension, or another time.

Tatjana Yurasova, former communications director of the *Siberian Installation*, was a covert operative for the elusive *Space Federation*. What little was known about the installation had created a shrouded mystery of speculation. The installation represented first contact of shamanic and extra-terrestrial light frequency, applied for enhancement and enlightenment potential of the Russian population.

There was a mystique around her presence and a legend about her source of knowing. She certainly commanded absolute respect in the Russian speaking world, as she had an uncanny gift of seeming to read the mind of the person she was interviewing.

She had questioned people as diverse as international chess champions, nuclear scientists, spiritual leaders, cosmonauts, as well as the President of Russia. Apart from being an interesting face among the amazing faces of the web of life, her fluency in many languages and mastery of diverse subjects – ranging from Aboriginal dream time to time travel –

had made her an instant celebrity. One of her most popular interviews was with her uncle, Vladimir Putin. She also interviewed Gorbatchev and the mysterious shaman from Turkmenistan, together discussing the fate of Russia, the spirits of trauma, and the supranatural world she identified as essential to first contact.

She had shown her command of economics during a key *Safe Place Earth* interview, when she invited eight central bank executives from around the world to discuss the derivatives markets and asked them, out in the open, to explain where the gold reserves of the G8 nations were stored.

One of her favourite and repeatedly debated subjects was the issue of safe places through major earth change scenarios. She frequently asked cosmologists, futurists and geologists to elaborate on the increasing frequency and intensity of earth quakes, volcanic eruptions, hurricanes and typhoons.

Tatjana Yurasova had clued in her viewers on all the really major relevant issue facing the world, giving them the type of background knowledge no one in the Western media would allow to be shown, let alone discussed openly. Her guests were in awe of her extensive knowledge, and at times somewhat fearful of her intense gift for getting the truth out.

In one noted segment she had grilled Al Gore about his alliances with Clinton and the New World Order, and she had tried to find out who financed the scientific *Global Warming* studies he represented. She had exposed one sitting US President about the hidden role of the US elections. She was highly respected as a real journalist and investigative reporter of the toughest kind, fiercely independent and free-spirited.

She had also questioned the Dalai Lama on his esoteric views, on the secrets of *The Nine*, rumoured to have existed thousands of years ago, and perhaps in control to this very day. Including their role in Burma, the regional expansions of

China and his views on the future of India.

She touched the issues surrounding the mysteries of the Tibetan rulers of the world, his dharma, and he surprisingly alluded to the possibility that his very own teachings could well be from other world contacts. She had invited Falun Dafa leaders to talk on her programme, and she made it clear that openness is all important. Her philosophy was, truth would always find its way, like a river finds its way to the sea.

Tatjana Yurasova made no secret of the fact that she consulted a top astrologer as to how to structure her popular shows, and on who to invite, and when. Her astrologer gave advice in person, to her viewers, commenting on world affairs in his credited presentation *Closer to The Stars*.

Her show was keenly followed in Eastern Europe, Asia and across India. She was the rising star of the Eastern hemisphere. Her high quality journalism was discussed on numerous leading internet web sites. However, she had not found a meaningful TV coverage in the Western hemisphere or even in Western Europe – areas that had completely blocked her *Safe Place Earth* show. This was destined to change, literally over night, when her interview with the Master of The Light was broadcast.

5
The Art of Seeing

"They walked on the bones of their own future ancestors."

~ Dr. Dan Burisch

The intrusion into our time line using a reality event distortion technology had begun to alter the behaviour of humans on the original time line by 2001. Global events were manipulated to create a convergence between the original time line and the anti-reality.

Just as the reality distortion moved to wipe out the cultural meditation of the Tibetans and the European Celts, they later began the next phase. Meditating Buddhist monks became the biggest obstacle to altering the path of the original time line on earth.

The studio was silent as Tatjana Yurasova began her opening statement, "People see what is happening around the world. Some events include lands under water, nuclear conflagrations, designer illnesses. Therefore, people ask where is it safe? Will Russia survive? Is the economic crash the cause of social decline? What is my purpose on earth at this time? Well, tonight we may find the answers to many of these questions. And I am happy to ask my special guest these and many more questions. Sir it is an honour to have you here, please tell us, is foreseeing the future possible at all?"

The Master of The Light answered, in his slightly other world accent, with an engaging smile that seemed both unmoved and ageless.

"The future surveyed by my group of remote seers is one of many probable futures that potentially lie ahead."

"If I may ask," Tatjana interjected. "What do you mean by probable futures?"

"The actual unfolding events determine which future this world takes. There are other probable futures which are all active and just as valid," answered The Master of The Light.

"Has your seer group seen a potential nuclear disaster in the years ahead of us?" she asked.

"The extreme future of a nuclear event is not active at this time," he said, looking briefly at his *SpaceStar* watch. "The events that would create that future by 2021 have not unfolded, and they probably will not unfold as is described by misguided observers. Our future reality is more alluring and stable than people today may think."

"Why do you say that we still have the potential to move away from the worst possible future at this time?"

"When Pluto entered Capricorn for the first time in over two hundred and fifty years, we realized the necessity of extracting ourselves from an alien-imposed anti-reality."

"When you say alien do you also mean paranormal?"

"The paranormal is a lesser form of intelligence. Essentially, the alien agenda includes intrusive paranormal events that are not part of our current reality."

"Do they look like us?"

"One type of alien appears to be human," he confided, "while others look like ghostly apparitions. Extra-terrestrials, who arrived when Pluto was in Gemini, in 1905, have not been idle. Do not assume that earth scientists develop their own theories. In fact, their agenda is manipulated by regressive aliens that intend to replace humans with clones. To control mankind, they are attempting to destroy the human spirit, science and high culture."

" I hear the wind blowing across the desert and I see the moons of a winter night rising like great ships in the void. To them I make my vow: I will be resolute and make an art of government; I will balance my inherited past and become a perfect storehouse of my relic memories. And I will be known for kindliness more than for knowledge. My face will shine down the corridors of time for as long as humans exist.

~ Frank Herbert,
Children of Dune

6
Leaving The Maze

The Master of The Light then spoke at length.

"Before we go any further into the complexities of extra-terrestrial origins and their manipulations of human events, we must consider something else of even greater importance. Human understanding of events happening around the world touches on one percent of what is really going on. Ninety-nine percent remains beyond the currents of human visibility, hidden in what is for now a cosmic mystery of non disclosed wisdom we have yet to awaken.

"What we see in this physical world today is what one might call the maze of events, and so it is not very conducive really to personal enlightenment to ponder if this or that faction, or group, nation or ET race gets the upper hand. I understand that your viewers have a right to know the truth, but the truth lies within individual consciousness and not outside in the labyrinth of accusations and denials.

"Within four generations, by the time Pluto moves from Pisces to Aries, the human species will be a unified teacher group and part of a new civilization, functioning as an awakened genetic and all-encompassing mind within a non-hierarchical structure. We come from a timeless lineage of advanced teachers representing a balanced inter-planetary culture, and when we tap into our intuitive intelligence, these things are known to us instantly. The new mind of mankind will become stable and with it able to use this knowing.

"Human beings today, and their perceived leaders, are not in charge nor in control of what goes on here on earth. This is something people need to be aware of. The regressive alien agenda is to control the natural progression of energetic human development.

"We want to leave *the maze* of this planet intellectually and spiritually speaking, to see beyond it and to foresee what really matters to mankind. We must remain unaffected by artificially constructed events that are hitting the world, so as to regain the inner ability of seeing, by which I mean seeing clearly.

What is really important – in addition to what *Jiddu Krishnamurti* taught – is that off planet groups are attempting to influence world leaders and sovereign nations; and only when each human being can overcome his or her own internal division will war and conflict end. You wish to know about extra-terrestrial contact, and what it is really all about."

She nodded and said, "I would like you to explore the notions of time travel, inner visions, and the techniques of remote seeing, and how you know what you know. But first let me quote Dr. Gerry Zeitlin, the former American scientist, who wrote in *OpenSETI*:

"In the twentieth century we broke our earthly bounds and walked the sky. In the twenty-first century we will seek companions there. Through science we hope to gain advance knowledge of who we will find.

The program designated to gain this advance knowledge is named The Search for Extra-terrestrial Intelligence. But SETI is nothing more than a badly-contrived myth. It seeks legitimacy through claiming membership in the larger scientific community, which itself is a collection of old myths that have outlived their usefulness.

You have suspected as much. Now for the first time, this issue is fully explained. Perhaps the SETI cheerleaders were your introduction to this subject.

Prepare now to go where they will not and cannot go – to where myth, mind, physics, consciousness and reality all meet. This subject demands no less. You deserve no less. The journey is crucially important – especially now, as we face the oncoming wave of chaos."

"An attempt at visualizing the Fourth Dimension: Take a point, stretch it into a line, curl it into a circle, twist it into a sphere, and punch through the sphere."

~ Albert Einstein

7
Seers, Prophets & Visionaries

"I take it you and most of your viewers have seen the videos with *Dr. Dan Burisch*, the former MJ12 micro-biologist of the Greys notorious *Area 51*, circulated on the internet in 2007.

"Human beings emerged on earth, from other worlds and other time dimensions, through highly advanced connections that span Cosmos. The higher civilisations call this the womb of life.

"Not all genetic variations on earth appeared out of the skies during extra-terrestrial interactions. The most ancient of earth's Egyptian civilisations were time travellers, as you would call them. They knew how to pass through the portals between the worlds. Your creator is a high-tech genius in terms of creating living mythology models of existence with interconnecting quantum fields.

"Space is an inhospitable supranatural place, not conducive to interstellar travel. Physical-biological life forms cannot survive outside the resonant field of their planetary sphere. The ancients had other ways to populate the earth, and other planets, with their cultural and racial seed."

"Are you saying that extra-terrestrial contact has formed the behaviour of cultures on our planet?" she asked.

"As you probably know, Mikhail Gorbatchev witnessed the extra-terrestrial connection in 1984. This is probably part of the reason he was able to sail the Glasnost ship so close to the wind within Russia, at that time.

"An offer of peace was rejected by the would be masters of the planet, since they believed that they held the upper hand, in terms of technology. The forces manifesting peace on the planet are very resourceful.

"The earth has been a hotspot for struggle and control over many millennia. The creative Cosmic experiment on earth is not an easy one for its inhabitants, at this time. Different races in conflict outside the earth have to get on. They have to learn to cooperate and understand each other. For their own survival and sanity, they have to learn to live together and appreciate each others differences.

"Outside the earth many of these races have an age old conflict raging, and in some cases these have created destructive interplanetary wars of the worst kind.

"The earth experiment was created to bring the warring races together and form an alliance of peace. Earth humans will one day be *Interplanetary Peacemakers*. Some of the more aggressive races do not want this, and their opposition makes its way into many governments and nations on earth."

"The conflict divides the different realms within the earth's magnetic field. In the near future people will connect with the different realities and learn from them again.

"These other realm contacts formed the mythologies of the ancient world, however, they are more real than people today can imagine."

"What you are saying sounds a bit like Tolkien's *Lord of The Rings*," She interjected, "This is also similar to the ancient shamanic circles of wisdom."

"Tolkien's world is more real than people want to understand at this time in earth's history. Humans were more connected in ancient times, but there was also less interference from the warring races.

"I have seen the assault on the Elves Kingdoms, the wars with the underground Dwarf races, the destruction of the older kingdoms and the closing of the energetic fields connecting the different vibrational realities on earth.

"I have lived through the genocide of the native peoples in North America, the destruction of the Toltec and Mayan kingdoms – and the ruin of Egypt. I have experienced the fall of Sumerian and far older Atlantean cultures who travelled from faraway stars in the *Orion* system.

51

"I have seen entire civilizations come and go; I was among those who sank Atlantis when we realized the experiment was running out of control. We used scalar technology.

"Today we have seen the North Atlantic sea passage open for shipping, and what does Canada do? They announce they wish to control the passage! As you see the insanity is still alive in terms of who wants to control the world's resources."

"It sounds like a dictatorship of the seas."

"The granite mountains of the countries will survive, as all dictatorships naturally come to an end, one way or another. From a Nordic, Tibetan or Celtic perspective the Art of Seeing is Zen applied. Meditation is, by far, the most elusive and also the most dangerous of all the Arts.

"The *Seeing Arts* can be deceptive to those who do not understand the background frequencies of visions, and especially the subtle vibrations of the as yet unformed futures.

"To better explain a little more why people make so many mistakes when they see what they think is a vision of future events. Entangled minds and misguided psychism lead to para-visions, they are blinded by the paranormal world in the same way Saruman was mislead by Sauron.

"Networks of converging time-space lines, frequencies of many dimensions and alternative realities, simultaneously exist in the same energetic space, all of them super-imposed on the unifying cosmic energies – the sea of frequencies we call life. Many different future realities co-exist, not all of them co-create.

"This means there are other options, other realities coming into the visual sphere of psychic human interactions. Clairvoyants often misunderstand the perceptions of these diverging time lines as their most probable future. Much later the events do not happen and people are confused."

"The art of seeing is to know when one is seeing events

52

pertaining to the future, or to know when one is seeing a parallel reality. Interacting with probable futures that may or may not take form requires a high level of discernment.

"There are societies that exist in a separate alternative reality as we live our reality. There have been attempts made to influence human society, not by extra-terrestrial races. It is an intrusion by fragmented fourth dimensional entities. That was the case in Egypt in the time around 3,500 BCE, in Tibet in the 12th Century, and in France in the 13th century.

"The future for the Americas and Europe has not yet taken form in the sense of what will actually unfold. Many good things have taken place that indicates a sane future is still possible.

"You also have to understand that if a certain country becomes the future dark lord described in some highly negative predictions, the whole world will fall apart.

"You are saying this is not going to happen?" she asked.

"The journey of consciousness through the physical material planes of existence is part of how the eternal spirit learns to relate to Cosmos," he replied, "The dynamics of that journey are still to be understood by an infantile humanity, only just beginning to emerge from a somewhat dark age. In this state, the consciousness of man is seeing a blurry vision of his own future that does not bear much resemblance to what is actually taking place."

Tatjana Yurasova continued, "I want to ask you a question about safe places, and how you would advise people to live and stay sane, and do you see Russia as safe haven?"

"In some way the place does not matter. Tibet, Tasmania, Patagonia, the Arctic Circle – or any place of your choice – are neither safe nor unsafe places as such. The safest place is in your heart, but there are some places with special merit and this – he held up a copy of his own book *Zen of Stars* – serves as guidance to answer this question in greater depth than I can do here in this short time together.

"Yes Russia has a good chance of seeing through these changes in a clear headed and responsible manner, and the future of Russia is to be a light to the world.

"One place of interest is Switzerland, which is not only at the hub of world events, it is an ancient key point of planetary evolution. What do you think the Celts were doing there? There is no coincidence that this is the home of the Knights Templars.

"Later the elite of the Helvetic Celts led their people to the Northern Highlands and Islands of Scotland. Alchemists understood what they buried there. It still has not been found.

"If Switzerland falls, then the whole world falls with it. However, the planet earth has a significant contribution to make to the evolution of the human species."

"You also said that planetary alignments indicate an implosion of the old market economy."

"Yes, research shows that the old markets and the global economy are ready to implode. But this is not a bad thing when we consider it more deeply. Sane people will develop a new way of sharing resources.

"This has to do with where the karmic monstrosities of colonialism took place. And I can show you a global map of the Reptilian insanity. This history excludes almost the entire western hemisphere from the Falklands all the way up to Newfoundland as a safe place zone – it is all karmic."

She then asked, "Why do seers and prophets see such differing outcomes?"

"Most competent psychics see different and conflicting negative events, because they do not have the skills to understand or distinguish the finer points of merging quantum realities. For instance, they have not studied climatology or cosmology and many of them do not know what they are talking about. It is not enough to *see* visions and apparitions. The genuine remote seer has the ability to interact with the ancient teachers of the invisible realms.

"I come from the *High Council of the Nordic Elves*, where we distinguish reality and anti-reality. I was taught things no one here remembers. There are real time markers revealing *the way* of the global script. You can see whether the events unfold as physical reality or if they take different turns than foreseen."

He continued, "I have seen a very special future for Switzerland and also for Russia, and some parts of Europe, but of course certain forces on and off earth wish to destroy that possibility. There is a parasitic presence that cannot feed off a healthy mankind. These issues will have to be addressed by earth humans as they recover their dignity. When this happens Germany will again be a great spiritual centre, as it was at the time of the Celts. In America, approaching 2020, the Phoenix will rise again from the ashes of destruction.

"Opposing this revitalisation of mankind is a regressive Reptilian Grey agenda, seeking to create disorder by broadcasting psychotronic visions of the worst possible future into the psychic mind of man, artificially encoding that future into the unaware minds of ordinary people.

"The human mind is so full of distortion, so that it is hardly capable of seeing clearly, never mind seeing the future clearly. Reality is the unformed future inside the 13th consciousness that opens in 2013. When our time meets this paradigm shift so too do the early Inuits, Celts, Tibetans and the ancient Toltecs within their own time dimension. The shared dream of the circle of many nations has to be balanced at any point in time."

"Can you, as a visionary, change the future?"

"In essence, yes. That is *The Art of Seeing*, which requires the ability to act outside the predominant thoughts and conditioning. The Germans and the world call this, the predominant reality, the *Zeitgeist*. However, to see the new possibilities, and the details of multiple realities living side by side within the same astrological alignments, is what I am suggesting. From there, I propose we enact our own time travel.

"This is related to the higher science of *hyper-quantum physics*. The seeing happens with the third eye, a form of psychic recall, where the remote seer can look into and understand the physics of the universe. As usual the human vocabulary gets in the way of full comprehension.

"Remote seeing multiple futures teaches us how to understand and find the solution within the chosen reality. This is how we change the future. We observe what is, and our consciousness reports these observations back to our soul guidance while still on this plane. Our own inner guidance is our own self giving us direction from a time yet to be.

"Initiate time travellers have to first understand this basic rule of existence if they are to *successfully* navigate the corridors of time. Travelling into our future, our many incarnations create a timeless tapestry of life, in which the soul is the weaver, and our incarnations are the threads of the fabric in which we clothe our spirit."

"In your book in which you wrote all the relevant advice and time coded trend predictions until 2050, you essentially suggested that we ought to protect our own minds in light of what has yet to transpire during the coming decades. Can you explain your notions of psychic mind protection and your breakthroughs in *NewMind Technologies*?"

8
NewMind Technologies

"Thought shattering itself
Against its own nothingness
Is the explosion of meditation."

~ Krishnamurti

Our team, in *Chillon Castle*, watched the projected holographic screen as The Master of The Light answered the many questions put to him by Tatjana Yurasova during her masterful interview. The view over the lake, in a different time, would have reflected the small lights of the French towns on the opposite shores of *Lac Leman*. In our future time meeting, with observers present from the *Galactic* and *Space Federations*, the water across *Chillon* reflected only the dark form of the silent mountains – our guardians of time.

I gave the scientists in the grand hall the astrological timing context to the following exchange of ideas during his interview, which had begun, after a few minutes, to resemble a dream within a dream.

Safely protected within the underground studio just outside Moscow, *The Master of The Light* began to outline the notions, including the futuristic concepts behind the science of time travel.

"NewMind Technologies and psychic mind protection involves a clear understanding of what planetary alignments suggest for mankind in the 21st Century."

"What do the planets and stars suggest according to your visionary analysis?"

"The arrival of the outermost planet of our solar system in 2009 into the sign that rules time and structure, society and governments, heralded a complete overhaul of everything to do with structural society as we know it.

"What does this entail? This is the subject of your Star Codex book, *Zen of Stars – Futures of Planet Earth*."

"Although we can track Pluto back every 250 years in the sign of Capricorn, and in theory we can look at the cycles of changes that occur each time the planet of transformation reaches the sign ruling societal structure, nothing in known human history compares with what we will witness by 2024. There is a vast test ahead for mankind.

"The events on the horizon are most probably to be seen as symptoms of a far deeper inner change that our species is entering into now. 2012 is widely seen as an important time marker. Much has been said about *2012*, but most of it is fear-based. An advanced astrologer sees this as a mere transition point among many, in a zone leading to 2047. There will be no singular event we can single out as a cause for many of the future changes. They had already begun a while back, and will reach a climax during the time Uranus and Pluto oppose in 2047. New and amazing abilities are on the horizon among the positive changes foreseen.

"Once the planet's population reaches the ability of global seeing and communication, which I refer to as time travel and *NewMind Technologies*, those who can apply the new mind will seek to create a structure which unifies world populations with civilizations living on other planets. This naturally implies that by then we know of the existence of those other cultures. During this time we also witness climate changes, bringing security issues that we address without fear. The dampening effect of the so-called *terrorist network* is to curb the will of the population to unify."

"Once this unification of the human mind group – via *NewMind Technologies* – is established, the population will be better able to cooperate, peacefully sharing resources and high tech knowing that come from extra-terrestrial discoveries awaiting mankind. Unification as such is not a bad thing. It is only dreaded by those who fear that control and their roots are taken away from them.

"The leadership of the current paradigm does not share this perspective, because their systems of reference are designed to protect the self interest established by previous generations, rather than to understand the broader context as it relates to the vital discoveries that lie ahead.

"Uranus – the planet associated with awakening, liberation, enlightenment, and often seen also as an omen of disruptive events – is making very challenging aspects to other outer planets until 2050. The tracking of Uranus represents really the unforeseen and the unexpected."

Tatjana then asked, "I read in *Zen of Stars* that you said the French Revolution and the Boxer Rebellion in China happened under similar alignments, I am sure the viewers would like to know if this scenario is about to repeat itself... Can you say something about this?"

"The king of France was executed in a Pluto Uranus opposition. So, it is to be expected that the unification of the species will not come about peacefully. Yet it will not hinder the world's progression to unify as a civilization, but rather, this will speed up its intended realization.

"Unfortunately, fear oddly produces unity out of necessity, in the long run. While sacrifices are required, it will generate a new sense of collective purpose and connection among the nations and tribes of earth – and also between all the races of our beautiful Cosmos."

"This sounds quite exciting as well as frightening. What then can I as a person do about this?" she asked.

"As to where you fit into this, Tatjana? If you remain fixed in the media-defined script of this dramatic story as it follows its ridiculous narrative all over the globe, instead of asking your own anticipatory skills for advice, you may be misguided to think and act as the world leaders do, which is centred on the protection of the self-interests of the so-called free world. Ask yourself! How free is this world really?"

"You may instead choose to rely more on the leadership and guidance of your inmost or future and higher self during the times to come, and place the disruptive and yet enlightening as well as awakening events in the broader context of the journey ahead – both for you as an individual and for humanity as a whole."

"Uranus is the most surprising of bringer of form. When he gets into another argument with an outer planet, strange things can happen. Is that right?"

The Master of The Light began to address himself directly to the viewers.

"Each of you feels as if you have walked unwittingly through a magical gate and, having seen what's on the other side, you want to return from whence you came, but the gate has locked behind you by now. You have passed a point of no return without knowing you did so... and so you ask, *well... what now?*"

"We have entered a new era where our vulnerability has been shown openly to us. Where are we really from? Who are the other races in space and what do they want here?"

"In reality, what lies ahead is not of conscious design, but rather a result of our accumulated ignorance of the *Cosmic Law* and its plans for us, and of our not knowing our own navigational guidance network; and subconsciously, there are few on planet Earth who do not realize all this. It is fair to say everyone knows deep down that we have been waiting for the allies of mankind for most of our whole collective lives, life time after life time. And now the time is upon us. We have arrived.

"No one is to blame for this condition of ignorance, mankind is being mankind. There is an evolutionary element unfolding within a long process of allowing the humanoid species to achieve the scientific discovery of the higher dimensions from which all life is woven. *The Nordic Blonds*, the *Andromedans* and their *Pleiadian* allies made these discoveries long ago, as did the *Sirians*, albeit long ago is to them what to us is our faraway future."

"What is our faraway future?" she asked.

"It is multi-dimensional. This timeless journey of mankind originated from the stars. The hidden encoded purpose is finding its way forward, to its ultimate goal, and it is this purpose that now seeks to articulate itself in the hearts and minds of all of you who are incarnate at this time and watching this interview.

"The discovery of man's ability to time travel will open the door to even more wonderful discoveries about the human soul and the true purpose of mankind.

"Ahead of this, *NewMind Technologies* is activating a more ancient discovery that does not require physical technology, other than the human mind.

"However, the mind that is able to make use of this inner purpose has to come face to face with its own stillness. Like a deep pool of water, untouched by the currents and ripples of time, the still mind conveys to the individual the essential purpose and instills in them an understanding of their place in that purpose.

"This was the essential meaning of the Tao, and those Taoists who successfully applied this stillness were, and still are, accomplished time travellers.

"The newly awakened mind will understand the depths of its own roots, and beyond. People will awaken to their purpose. The mind is the key, the physical technology follows after.

"There will be many new and some very severe tests that will assail humanity throughout the 21st century. Some of the changes will be more profoundly earth shaking and much more personally uprooting. However, we can track these tests ahead of time via the alignments the planets quite clearly make to one another.

"World leaders will draw an artificial line between good and evil and seek to eradicate the evil, and in every instance the target will only extend further and further into the deep recesses of obscurity and de-centralization. No physical technology can stop or advance this process.

"There is an ultimate strategy for all life-bearing planets. Like the Tao it is moving and changing in ways that can only make man wonder, and be inspired by the complexity of its design. The only stability inherent to the grand plan is the ultimate goal; the voyage itself weaves, accelerates, and sometimes even reverses in direction. The goal, as you might wonder about it, is to create a highly advanced being who can work with the force. It is the force that extends to mankind the capacity of time travel."

"I have here a quote that more accurately describes this process of unfragmented consciousness." He said as he began to read to the world.

"When we stop fighting with ourselves, we aren't creating anymore conflict in our mind. Then our mind can for the first time relax and be still. Then for the first time our consciousness can become whole and unfragmented. Then total attention can be given to all of our thoughts and feelings. And then there will be found a gentleness and a goodness in us that can embrace all that is been given in the world. Then a deep love for everything will be the result of this deep attention. For this total attention, this soft and pure consciousness that we are, is nothing but Love itself."

63

"This was by Krishnamurti, your own teacher and friend," Tatjana Yurasova added, "A truly amazing man... So, this concept you are introducing of action without thought, choiceless awareness and the ending of conflict you just quoted, can you elaborate more on the relevance of this to the current situation worldwide?"

"We are basically running out of time now, both on earth, and on this TV show. As the master of time Saturn dissolved its opposition to Neptune in 2007, worldly affairs received clarification. During the Saturn-Uranus opposition in 2009 we entered the phase of the actual countdown to 2013. This phase lasted one decade, the convergence zone, until about 2017/18 – 2012/13 being the mid point.

"The *social engineering* and *controlled disorder* techniques – legal black magic in the form of thought control used by secret governments all over the world – will become evident as the Pluto-Uranus square builds more tightly by the middle of 2015. By 2026, when Neptune enters Aries, things change at first very subtly – then, later, abruptly.

"It is indeed possible that entire lakes disappear overnight. Where flatlands once were, the next morning mountain ranges appear, and entire islands vanish, while land rises again from below the ocean. This will not only be due to massive quakes, it will happen because of inter-dimensional vortex holes in the fabric of reality. This phenomenon is typical of Neptune meets Saturn in 2025. Some of us will feel as if we entered a mirage or time portal. Pluto was in line of the Galactic Centre in 2006 when these time portals began opening in some undefined places, such as the mirages photographed in China after the typhoons. This Galactic Center event happens once every 250 years, and the last two windows in time were in 1760, when Halley comet was discovered, and in 1514, when Copernicus first observed Saturn, my home planet. It rules Capricorn."

"Capricorn rules time travel. It is the slice of Cosmos associated with trans-personal considerations, society as a whole, and we investigate the workings of inner governments and the subjects of hidden social manipulation – programs used by dark forces trying to rule the world in its melt down phase.

"As I predicted, there will be much more disclosure on many extremely interesting subjects, ranging from human hybrid genetics, reversed engineering, the hidden role of NASA, to alien sourced technology, and the true search for extra-terrestrial intelligence.

"This is something scientist *Dr. Gerry Zeitlin* has commented on for years, after the first book by Anton Parks, *Le Secret Des Etoiles Sombres* appeared in France. The publishing and dissemination of new ideas is currently undergoing a major revolution.

"Before this, *The Morning of The Magicians*, presented similar revolutionized questions fifty years ago, and again it was France that led this information revolution in terms of free expression of thought. The disclosure is perhaps overlooked due to its simplicity: *"We came from the stars, and we are guiding ourselves back to the stars, from our own future.*

"Planet earth is not our original home. Until now we have shared the planet with fallen races that managed to enslave mankind, and we will soon leave them behind as the earth cleans up the resulting mess."

At *NORAD's Strategic Space Command Centre SSCC* in Wyoming the phones did not work; military installations had gone dark, and around all global communications networks pandemonium had broken out, as Tatjana Yurasova's *Safe Place Earth* appeared mysteriously all over the TV network broadcasting systems worldwide.

At the same time thousands of disk shaped space crafts had been sighted over towns and cities all over the world. No one connected to the media system had dared to officially report this phenomenon. It was a standing joke between dedicated researchers about mass media versus reality. Millions of people in all countries were bypassing the censorship, as they shared the mass sightings news, sending photos and videos via i-phones and blackberries. The Internet was broadcasting coverage of the daylight phenomena, as craft appeared – brightly lit – over the city of Moscow.

Tatjana resumed her interview unfazed as news of the sightings was flooding in. "Can you give me an outline of what will actually happen in both the inner mind landscape and the outer world as society comes to terms with this mysterious reality we are now witnessing around the world?"

The Master of The Light chose his words carefully, speaking with measured intent. "The mirror between the inner state of mind and the outer manifestation of world events is the subtle way in which we can see the actual developmental stage of mankind, and in turn, this activity is mirrored by the planets, making it readable ahead of its time.

"*How* people observe the strange phenomenon manifesting now on planet earth is more important than the phenomenon itself. Human beings will eventually come to understand that they themselves are *inwardly* part of the outer phenomenon they are observing. When humans comprehend this subtle truth they will instantly become masters of their own reality."

The studio broadcast cut to images of the silent disks and cigar shaped crafts appearing in the skies, hovering far above the watching mind of man on planet earth.

9

The Unseen Conflict

World events were changing at such a pace, it was clear that leaders in governments and underground bases had little time left to tighten their control on global populations. Keeping disclosure material classified was paramount to maintaining control. It was with these questions in mind that investigative researcher *Kerry Lynn Cassidy*, of *Project Camelot*, approached the special team operating from the mysterious time portal at *Château Chillon*, to interview The Master of The Light.

The following *Project Camelot Interview* – called *Dragon Gold* – was a time travel masterpiece, outlining the *2012-Y2K* deception masterminded to take out the core intelligence of mankind before people woke up to the fact that, for centuries, the *Globalisation End Times* scenario had been designed to disinform society.

Kerry Cassidy returned to *Chillon* Castle to be met by representatives of *The Council*, and until today she refuses to say if she actually conducted the famed interview in her current time, or if she passed through the portal to meet the group in their own surroundings to film *Dragon Gold*.

It was no accident that the most popular clip viewed on *Google Video* and *Project Camelot* websites outlined the key planetary factors behind *The Unseen Conflict*.

With the waters of Lac Leman shining through the tall windows, the Master of Light outlined the passage of time.

"From 2009 until 2024 Pluto is in Capricorn – with as its background factor from 2012 onwards Neptune in Pisces, simultaneous, until 2026. This means many exciting things are in the making now. The most important societal movements of the recent past began while the U.S.A. paperwork was signed in 1776 when Pluto was in Capricorn, and the development of what we know as America, its history and our modern existence, unfolded within this last Pluto cycle.

"However, the whole story began with the extermination of

the Native American Indians. The events – tangentially speaking – can be understood in historical terms as *"the first step is the last step."* Societal and industrial developments started around 1760 have now run their full course. America began with violence and deception, and the society developed this relationship with the rest of the world. Violence breeds conflict, and so on."

"Where does the Mayan calculation fit into all this?"

"The Mayan calendar *supposedly* identifies 2012 as the last moment in time, but one has to know that astrologically, sometime between Venus cycles 2012, 2020 and 2028, the actual end game takes place. The Mayans were quoted out of context by regressives who tried already in 1999 to put fear into mankind with *Y2K*. In that sense *2012* is not what it was said to be. After 2012, a new target date will be invented to create a new fear. *9/11* was a typical *controlled disorder* operation, as was the *avian flu*.

"Geopolitical changes are planned, as we will see when this reality show resumes. Power does initially concentrate in the hands of the few so-called super-powerful and super-rich, until all of it implodes around 2020. Again, the first step is the last step. Keep in mind that no civilization is conquered from outside until and unless it has been rotting long enough from inside. To see this through, all you need to do is know *how* to wait.

"Fear of secret enemies and their hidden governments immobilizes mankind. By 2020 when Saturn passes in line of Pluto in Capricorn, sign ruled by Saturn, things change. State and corporate leadership and their plutocratic governments become oppressive under this influence, and consequently, one is advised to anticipate more police state type developments in the Western world, but also equally powerful, albeit secretive, underground factions to rebel.

"America's *9/11* was one such signal to the would be controllers, but this has so far eluded mankind. Some suggest that this was an alien take over attempt that failed miserably.

"This trend is indicated also because of the challenging alignment made by Uranus to Pluto from 2012-2017, and that includes the *state within the state* factions and militia groups, as well as ordinary citizens' movements. These developments will show world-wide, not only inside America. Europe, Russia. First and foremost China and India are also ripe for extreme transformations from within. South America fares better because they are shifting over gently to guided leadership by their shamanistic cultures. Order comes from living aligned to the laws of Cosmos, not by manmade rules.

"The patterns mirror, some say caused, things like the thirteen American founding colonies to rebel against Britain in 1764, after Pluto last entered Capricorn, when Uranus was in Aries, which created this compelling popular force urging chaotically for freedom and independence. The exact same configuration signature shows from *2012-2017*, which is the time I consider to be dangerous and enlightening.

"These explosive planetary energies are the most defining transit influence for the coming decade, bringing the societal, cultural, economic, scientific, political, and military revolutions that began in 1965/66 under a Pluto-Uranus conjunction into the next phase, until that syndrome resolves around 2047/48 when Uranus opposes Pluto."

"Everything birthed in the mid Sixties is bound to take quantum leaps forward, such as movements for social justice, civil rights, paradigm-busting technologies like i-phones and the management of human genetics or the world-wide eco-systems. Now is the time not only to envision, but to begin instantly manifesting the results we wish to see, to make miracles happen in our personal lives – a thing for which we are DNA wired; a period demonstrating quite a volatile energy full of fundamental transformative event zones."

"All this comes on the heels of the long standing Saturn-Neptune and Saturn-Uranus oppositions, which are indicative of tectonic shifts, tsunamis, earth movements, water shortages, replacement of oil as a source of energy, and all the themes associated with sustainable living and envisioning new energy solutions.

"If we look at Saturn as manifestation planet and bringer of form to disciplines of functionality, frugality, logic, places of retreats and restraint, in constructive aspects to Capricorn awareness – expanding this theme usefully – then we see that the window of time is well starred for ventures dealing with solving the problems we perceive.

"Once Pluto settles into Aquarius past 2024 and until 2044, events turn towards transformations of earth and humanity as a fully networked society. Usefulness of systems management becomes the key concern. Saturn opposes Pluto in 2036 when tensions arise. Pluto and Neptune – always seen as a couple – do suggest that on the whole, as a society, we move from fear based thinking to a more conducive behaviour of ethical cooperation among tribes and races over the next four decades.

"The time lines shown by my astrology suggest a high degree of caution is indicated for a window between 2.22.2009 and 8.8.2013 – a moment bridging a phase in which many forces align for a potentially explosive as well as exciting denouement. This leads to the question pertaining to the mega trends. You have three key zones, and they are going to be the years of 2017, 2027 and 2047. What are they actually about? First of all comes what I call *NewMind Technologies*, then *The 13th Consciousness* – and the paramount *First Soul Contact*. But that's for 2017."

"The first step is the last step. No civilization is conquered from outside unless it has been rotting long enough from inside. Techno-Spirituality is to know how to follow the bright Light."

~ Michael St.Clair

10
First Soul Contact

The grand hall of *Chillon* was silent, and it seemed as if eight hundred years echoed with the presence of the advanced souls who had designed the Celtic fortress. A timeless stillness permeated the stone walls. *Kerry Lynn Cassidy* and *The Master of The Light* sat peacefully talking at the visionary windows looking out onto the lake.

"Take me beyond 2012. What scenarios do you foresee for the 21st Century? I know you relate the condition of the new mind to the future outcome of first soul contact."

"*The 13th Consciousness Activation* phase beginning in 2013 opens a window of wisdom beyond any teaching, Tao excluded, as it encompasses all living organisms in Cosmos," he began to outline.

"The seekers who share their knowing are noble, by virtue of their open-ended quest for the truth, and as they respect their own evolution of assimilating new concepts, always honouring universal or *Cosmic Intelligence* much more than the mere indoctrination or conditioning part of any system, method or teaching of any kind and of any source.

"Some rare teachings, however, came from beyond the space time continuum and can serve as guidance. *The Tao* is one. The concepts shown by *The WingMakers* are another one. The ideas shown by *The Master of The Light* are worth looking into, when applied properly. *Jiddu Krishnamurti* taught: *Action without thought.*

"These are, however, not teachings per se. They are *pointers* in a different or untried direction, timeless, so as to help a seeker to see anew, which is what *Aries Uranus* would suggest we do by 2012 – activating our own time travel ability as a living technology from within our own third eye.

"There will soon be an irrefutable explanation for – and scientific discovery of – the human soul, and an uncovering of what this means for all of us, sometime between 2024 and

2048. There will come with it the realization that we are quantum fields within quantum fields, able to see and connect willingly with *The Guidance of Cosmic Intelligence.*

"Some of us are testing this and have done so for years already. Yes, some of us are involved in highly advanced and discreet projects beyond the clearance level of the most classified materials available. Heads of states are, by virtue of their lower level jobs, underneath this clearance level.

"It is a monumental master type event of which mankind has been dreaming for many millennia, to be able to take our proper space in the bigger scheme of things, and to act as miniature creators within creation itself. As Jupiter will meet Pluto and Saturn in Capricorn in December 2020, we will see how far we have progressed in this realization of re-incarnated truth. The next check-point is in 2048.

"Some researchers see the discovery associated with the arrival of time travel as more likely by 2060 or 2080, but I am of a more optimistic spirit as some of us have already found out for ourselves how close we are to the thinning veils and new passageways ahead. We have seen the opening doorways of the soul, and have visited other invisible worlds of higher frequencies, while some of us have actually journeyed to the alternative earth planets.

"This will show us that mankind is not an isolated or coincidental experiment of Creation, but rather part of an amazingly multi-faceted and diverse coordination of intelligent and guided life – one that spans multiple universes and many more dimensions and warp spaces than we can fathom right now. But we will be able to experience all of it very soon, minus the mental conditioning, minus the greed, and most importantly, minus the secrecy."

"What does *First Contact* mean in your opinion?"

"*First Contact* means first hand or first soul experience.

The old brain thought structures and belief systems – thought and belief are fear-based – will try to create walls around the new knowledge we will gain. The unknown will tend to scare established systems. But like the scarab of the Egyptians, we the more adventurous ones will move the knowing forward and use it well.

"The collective voyage of the seekers undergoes massive changes following the discovery of the integrated and newer sciences, such as our true cosmology, a new mathematics, the particle physics and a new molecular biology – as they will soon begin to completely restructure the planetary institutions of society, religion, government, philosophy, education, and high culture. Our friends from deep space have been patiently waiting for millennia for us to catch up with them.

"We will indeed experience the benefits of orgone energy, of time-travel, teleportation, anti-gravity, and much more to come. All these developments are overdue when Pluto traverses the trans-personal signs of the Zodiac – Capricorn, Aquarius and Pisces. By 2048, the impulse for change will be self-generated, and possibly quite violent, should progress for mankind have been hemmed in by the hostile alien presence. The desire is to break out, and break out we will.

"The discoveries that await us, and that we have been working for and evolving towards – for at least the past 12,000 years since Atlantis vanished – will change the destiny of this space vessel, the earth itself, for the better and forever. However, before we get to this, we have some house cleaning to attend to which entails disconnecting certain human cloned government structures from their alien handlers.

"Until then many readjustments are needed. The knowing was here all along – since Cosmos is a living library – and it is not really new. During this important time the knowledge will be re-discovered and then applied in functional ways.

"This can be exhilarating or deeply unsettling, right?"

"Depending on how evolved we are, yes. Going through some of the relevant check points in the *Galactic Clock*, we see certain dates that stand out. When reality meets surrealism in 2025 during the conjunction of Saturn and Neptune on the cusp of Pisces and Aries, we will meet the soul makers.

"A cycle ends, a new one opens. The place of action in this meeting between the planets ruling the real and unreal is in the cusp zone from Pisces to Aries – the 12th and 1st signs of the Zodiac – or the slice in the heavens known as the alpha and the omega, where eternal wisdom comes from. Zen masters see this as the point where merger and unity take place. Oneness comes there from experience of having seen and done it all.

"We want to stay absolutely non-aligned to systems or methods of spirituality, so as to be able to move with intellectual fluidity like dolphins in water when the new mind awakens, and it is about to awaken as we will see soon. Even this advanced kind of *NewMind Astrology* is now undergoing massive changes, and upgrades are due.

"The blessings of Pisces are intelligent and distant compassion coupled to enlightened disbelief. Pisces says to its fellow time travellers: *I see you there then – when you have also grasped it. Meanwhile I love you all.*

"Neptune – the planet ruling Pisces, dreams, psychism and inspirations – sails through the sign it holds sway over from February 2012 to March 2025, definitely dissolving the boundaries of thought and preparing an inauguration or passage of *zones of time* into the unseen realms of techno-spirituality."

"What do you mean by Techno-Spirituality?"

"Techno-Spirituality is a notion I created as it came to me by transliterating the planetary alignments in the times we engage into, and it means – as translated from Greek and from archaic pre-Sumerian or extra-terrestrial code languages: *"Know how to follow the bright light."*

"In early 2025 – what I term the apex of the age of techno-spirituality – Pluto will just have entered visionary Aquarius, making this phase past 2025 and until early 2044 a networked venture indeed, after years of testing what is of use or structurally valid in Capricorn. Time travel as a science will begin in earnest in 2025 and it will be taught at universities. *The Nordic Blonds* have been showing me the secret protocols of these teachings over the past years."

Kerry asked: "Do you see the *Nordic ETs* playing a major role on earth in the years ahead?"

"They have been a part of history since the beginning of our time on earth. Although their role in our development has remained largely hidden, parts of it lie encoded in sagas and ancient mythologies. Yes, they will play a decisive role now.

"The *Nordic Blonds* are an extremely advanced humanoid race that agreed not to wage wars, after they rid themselves of the *Greys* on several star systems. Over millennia, Nordic and other seers of perennial value have experienced diverse and difficult situations involving aliens from other worlds, such as the Romans invading the Celtic homelands, or the hunting down of the Knights Templars, the occupation of Tibet by China, the killing of the Beothuks in Newfoundland, and of the Burmese monks – yes and many other unwritten and atrocious histories similar to Tolkien's epic saga partly outlined in *The Lord of The Rings.*

"This ongoing saga is, in effect, a reality show in the making for the past five thousand years. *The Inuits* who were living around the arctic circle, from the Russian to the

Alaskan, Baffin Island, Greenland and other territories, the Aborigines in Australia, the Tibetans, the Toltecs, and the Natives in North America, and so many more, have seen it all. As have you and I."

"What do you see happening to change this in the decades ahead. I mean, many prophecies claim that humanity will reach some kind of planetary peace. Do you also see that happening?"

"In 2044 Pluto will be in the first degree of Pisces – the spot that Neptune engages into in early 2012. At this point we enter a phase manifesting the phrase, *"The meek will inherit the earth"*, which means instead of the elite being in charge of this earth, common people will manage and share its resources – as it is said that Pisces can muster meekness and with it fluidity and enlightened insights into the ways of the peaceful and shamanic archetypes.

"Thus the 21st century of our time sees this 12th or Pisces consciousness and its inherent mystery written very large over the firmament of the heavens. Until 2011, Uranus is in Pisces. You see, Uranus prepares this whole enlightenment potential of our new mankind, awakening the DNA of people to this Piscean music of the spheres, while Neptune will mystify and dissolve these matters, giving them new forms of formlessness, whereas Pluto will later transform them yet again, but much more radically so.

"Shape shifting the zones ahead from now until well into 2060 with agility and subtlety, when we ought to reach the acquisition of the blank slate technology... which is Awakening – Dissolution – Transformation – in that order: From 2012 to 2025 to 2048, and beyond.

"In 2025 Saturn will be conjunct Neptune for a while in the interesting switching zone of Pisces 30 and Aries 1, where the Alpha meets the Omega. Aries 1 has this suggestive Sabian symbol of *A Woman Just Risen from the Sea; A Seal Is Embracing Her* (keyword: Realization); whereas Pisces 30 has as its Sabian symbol this beautiful, and last of all the 360 degrees images:

A Majestic Rock Formation Resembling A Face – Idealized by a Boy who takes It as His Ideal of Greatness – and as He Grows Up, He Begins to Look Like It. (Keyword: Discernment)

"It is best not to interpret this further, but rather to meditate on the imagery, and to simply know this is the point in which form bringing reality of Saturn meet surrealism of Neptune. This Saturn-Neptune conjunction phase tells us that 2027 will be an era when ideals transform, when form and formlessness merge to begin something never tried. This is the moment of multiple paradigm shape-shifts, from what we entered into during the quest of Pluto in Capricorn, to the new realizations of our own origination, until we make first soul contact with the first cosmic source."

"Can you describe the first cosmic source, do you know it?"

"As you consider it deeply you see that separation and death is illusion. Some of us have already realized this aeons ago; and we have already seen our future, as we have certainty of inner guided knowing.

"We shall learn a lot more in one Uranus cycle or human life, when 2047 morphs into 2137. In its darkest light, first cosmic source, the *all that is*, created you and me from its intent to comprehend its own creation. We are therefore its ambassadors – free to journey through Cosmos as particles of its womb of life – with destinies only we alone can and will create. In that sense, the *Age of Time Travel* begins as we enter into and become one with the invisible worlds."

11
Invisible Worlds

"The unseen worlds will become visible. Due to their subtle frequencies other world vibrations have remained invisible to the physical eyes of man, yet this changes around 2025 when the bringer of form Saturn, as a reality master, moves in line of Neptune, the planet of dreams, illusions and mirages in the mysterious sign ruled by Neptune – Pisces.

"As the frequencies of our minds and bodies take on a lighter higher vibration, the brain will shift its energy to a state that makes it possible to see the unseeable.

"Neptune was discovered in 1846 when it was also just conjunct Saturn, in Aquarius – sign ruled by Uranus, when Uranus itself was in Aries, blazing a new trail and opening up the thought process of humanity in terms of science and mind connectivity. At least the mid 19th Century seemed like a new beginning, and in Russia you saw truly brilliant minds writing phenomenal pieces of literature. There was an atmosphere, during that time, of profound hope.

"The planetary inhabitants of the 19th Century had still quite a long way to go until they would see clearer, and so here we have again the phenomenon of reality meets surrealism – meaning a test of time, Saturn-Neptune, leading from illusion to reality, and from form to formlessness. This is a form of interdependent origination at its best.

"The 19th Century brought to light occult movements such as *The Golden Dawn*. Franz Anton Mesmer healed people using powerful magnets – and other things of this Uranian-Neptunian nature began to flourish then. Swiss born Mesmer believed that a kind of psychic ether pervades all space, and that the astral bodies cause tides in this fluid, or ether. Nikola Tesla and Wilhelm Reich worked with his findings one Uranus cycle later, only to be suppressed and killed.

"On a political societal level, also in 1846, the Communist Manifesto by Karl Marx was disseminated, proposed by the secret bankers of the world, and as you will see by 2048 we will be moving into a society that might be more tribal, more high tech, and totally interconnected with its space brothers, without relying on hierarchical teachings.

"By 2050 – when we experience a sense of calm, which Neptune, ruler of imagination develops in matters of spiritual cosmology and connectedness – we will understand extra-terrestrial intelligence and apply it. So far we had no clue about true cosmology, the origin of the universe, and we barely know where we come from.

"We live our lives based on what Gerry Zeitlin calls the SCAM – *Society's Common Approved Myth*. Yet we do not even honour let alone comprehend our ancient myths. In 1846 – a whole new science came along with Uranian inspiration and showed advanced frontiers.

"Now as then we will aim for early ubiquity, everywhere at once in the advanced stages. We know that we will soon reach the *ending of time* and the *end of thought*; and we will move by 2025 into *the time of limitless seeing* – when only direct knowledge will be of use, or of value. This silent knowing is to be taught also to the future leaders of our tribal nations. Those leaders will be totally different from what we have seen in the last few thousand years. In Russia you already see this happening." He said, pausing as Kerry responded.

"Well, Russia is highly advanced in these terms. I met young Boriska, who certainly has a lot of information about the extra-terrestrial context of what you say. In a short time, Vladimir Putin obviously changed direction."

"Yes," he continued, "Putin's legacy is a Russia that does not depend on the Western powers. In and by itself it is a masterful achievement. He knows how to use the mind in a balanced way. As was clear during his visit to the Shaolin Temple in the Henan Province, China, he is a diplomat with

Libra planets at birth, obviously able to mediate successfully between conflicting parties.

"This man of peace understood that his come back was to be engineered in two stages, after *The Great Game*. He will return, as he had clearly foreseen the *Persian Gambit*. He avoided the problem, leaving Western powers to deal with what they created, ages ago. He is a man of amazing intellectual elegance, trained by the ancient masters."

Kerry added, "I heard that Iran helped to oust Russia from Afghanistan, and was instrumental in leaving *CIA* asset Saddam Hussein in power. Essentially, it seems that Iran played a double game with the so-called super powers."

"Persia and Russia are brothers of the same tribe, who became ancient enemies." He answered, "This is a karmic conflict. The advanced Sufi mind would seek peace for all. This peace is not only about human beings, but it includes the peace of rivers, trees, mountains – the environment. That is a powerful Sufi philosophy which aligns with Zen."

"I take it that applies to the much talked about climate changes. There is a lot of confusion about what we are facing in terms of these problems." Kerry added.

"You see, the mass media play with simplistic notions designed to create fear and misunderstanding within the populations." He continued, "Industrial society has been polluting the planet from the mid 18th Century. The problem began with the mindset, let's rip-off the earth and burn everything down in the name of human progress. This approach is now two hundred years in the making. People were aware of the price being paid in terms of habitat degradation, and they went ahead anyway.

"The whole solar system is going through a change – there have always been changes. This discussion of whether mankind produces global warming is irrelevant. The issue is, are we going to act like pirates and take what we can? The problem is we are also dealing with questions of resource scarcity, and this always leads to conflict and wars – and wars are the biggest contributors to global pollution.

"Each one of us in the council of time lords – ambassadors between different warring races – have their own specialties and missions. Climatology is one for climatologists, and my expertise is cosmic time travel. Each of us knows the point in each of our incarnations where we must interface with destiny if we are at all serious about setting the priorities in our own lives.

"With respect to time travel, climate changes is about how each of us responds to ages of chaos. Once more, it is not so much the outer phenomenon that needs our attention and focus, but it is the inner response that is vital when meeting these issues. The inner response creates the human future.

"It is important to understand that the general mass alarm has nothing to do with addressing what is truly happening. The world bank and similar global institutions are financing the destruction of the planet. So called bio-fuel is already being used to extract protected resources from areas now under siege. Global consumption has become a disease."

Kerry asked, "How do you relate all of this to time travel?"

"Through the ability to perceive where we are going in terms of the worst possible future, an aware and forewarned humanity can change the future outcome by changing direction. In this sense time travel is a mental, almost psychic exercise. Know where the dangers are, and you may not go there. Krishnamurti called this choiceless awareness.

"I studied Krishnamurti's teachings, and I know where you are coming from." She added.

"Unless human beings have a sane, healthy relationship with the land they live on, they act in ways that destroy their

85

own future. Similarly, without respecting our own selves we will not respect the earth.

"It is important to establish a relationship to our own guidance. In terms of the time traveller awareness this guidance comes from our own future selves. Using the mind, or the *Guidance* from within, right action is achieved, while paying careful attention to the living signs our environment gives us on a daily basis.

"By living signs I mean the simple shamanic or seemingly random little things we can pick up every day when walking around, in a forest while observing animals, or in a crowded city street while paying attention to people, provided we are awake and alert to even do that.

"In terms of my work this also includes a living mind technology. When scientists use the mind of the seer they will find the solution.

"The problems facing mankind are not of a runaway planet out of control, but are related to the flawed state of our minds. The unseen reality is that the earth is protecting itself and us with it, although the eco-system is currently in a state of upheaval and collapse.

"There are key points in the solar system and galactic orbits where things change, complete transformation occurs and the magnetic frequency of the earth is forever altered. It is not only earth that undergoes alterations, but the sun and all the planets known to our scientists experience similar cyclical changes.

"*The Space Federation* have reported observing the effects of storms on Uranus, Saturn, Jupiter, Triton and Mars, and many other orbiting bodies in our solar system. There have also been magnetic field changes.

"It is not correct to say that mankind is the cause of, or responsible for creating the current climate change. It is, however, equally incorrect for humans to think they can continue to pollute, and literally destroy the earth they walk upon. Future generations will be effected by how we walk on the surface of the earth today.

"The process of planetary change is natural. This cycle of change will happen regardless of the ecological situation on planet Earth. The decisive and fundamental problem for mankind is its own collective state of mind. Human beings are not in danger from the planet they inhabit; they are a danger to themselves. In that respect people are totally out of step with the cycle now unfolding."

"I know that you have been warning people, for many years already, about powerful earthquakes, devastating storms, catastrophes, flooding. How is that different from the general information seeping into society now?" she asked.

"When I began to warn people in 1999 that catastrophic changes would alter the earth, I also pointed out the solutions, such as the constructive use of hemp for building, for clothing, for heating, for food, medicine, and much more.

"In addition, I showed people something empowering, which is the value of our lives as we enter this new and exciting time. *Krishnamurti* spent sixty years teaching people what they can do to transform relationship. He said in essence, *End the problem maker.*

"Obviously, the problem maker, thought, will not create the solutions needed to see through these diverse times ahead. The ending of thought and the activation of source intelligence creates a totally new mind. Only this new mind will find the solutions successfully and sail the seas of tomorrow.

"That was very poetically said," added Kerry. "And so, how do you see us sailing the seas of tomorrow?" she asked.

"The quality of human experience," he answered, "has largely degenerated at a time when people need to be highly alert and sensitive to instant change. Using the living technology of inner seeing, and psychic time travel, is something the people in ancient times knew how to do. Those who lacked this ability then were regarded as being unwell, whereas today the few who have this ability are feared. This is the real problem facing society, and not so much the natural events unfolding in this time. Mankind is in for a reawakening to its own potential as well as to the restructuring of its own thought patterns.

"As bad as things appear in terms of physical human pollution and the ecological deterioration of the environment, the real disturbance is the psychic and psychological pollution. The degraded way humans think and behave is far more toxic than the physical pollution. Wilhelm Reich addressed this in his discovery of orgone and in his development of the orgone generators. He also paid the ultimate price for his brilliant inventiveness and knowing.

"The inner disturbance of the collective psyche disables the human capacity to cope with the challenges of the next five decades. Our way of thinking is a far greater danger to us than the *Earth Changes*; but no one wants to seriously address any of this."

"Why?"

"Because this would entail a much deeper personal change of behaviour. In the future, this is how mankind can save the environment. The situation at this time of cyclical change in the magnetic field of the solar system and on earth means that the support and stability of the natural environment is not something we can rely on. During planetary upheaval, how can a severely damaged environment protect and nourish us when we have destroyed most of it? This is the issue we are facing now as the earth begins to dramatically alter its resonance.

"That touches on the Hopi message," Kerry interrupted,

"where the Native American Elders have said we made choices that have led to the spiritual degeneration of mankind."

"Yes, this goes all the way back to the destruction of the native indigenous cultures living in harmony with the earth." he agreed. "The *Inuits* living close to the Arctic know what this means in terms of a complete change in their way of life, as the ice caps melt.

"We must think about how the so-called civilized cultures treated the ancient cultures, and perhaps learn to respect their wisdom. The technological cultures have an interest in learning from them, as they will be the survivors. The issues facing humans on this planet are related to our learning ability and not the weather changes."

"There is also the question," Kerry added, "of HAARP, the artificial weather modification experiments, the Chemtrail spraying and the idea that the secret government has a goal to control the weather by 2025. Doesn't this have a part to play in the global chaotic weather?"

"These experiments are part of the insane mind." He answered. "This is why I say that it all comes back to the consciousness of mankind. I know that alien governments are altering the weather. This activity is being carefully monitored by the Galactic Federation.

"Do you want to say something more about the Galactic Federation at this point?" she asked.

"No I do not," he answered, "I have nothing more to add, at this point. The collective human consciousness allows it, for their own misguided reasons."

"We are leaving the times of abundance and we are entering longer stretches of stark scarcity. How we adapt to this new paradigm is going to define our collective future. The self indulgent greed based societies will not be able to cope mentally with the harsh reality they are about to face. Rather than look outside and grow fearful, we must take a good look in the mirror and realign our personalities and priorities. Who are we, really, and why are we here? A mind that cannot contain its greed will create conflict at a time when it has to share equally with others.

"Perhaps it is time that we learn true compassion for our surrounding environment, for the animals, rocks, plants and trees. Planet earth is giving birth to a new mind, at the same time humans are devouring the planet. During this self-destructive process we are killing ourselves. The natural environment is rapidly disappearing. This insanity has to be addressed if the human race is to survive and continue.

"The cause of this destruction lies inside the human mind. That is the central issue of my prediction. The human mind faces its own natural tsunami, which is not to focus outside, but to be aware of what is going on inside. The enveloping wave is a wave of energy, of consciousness."

"Describe to me your vision of the 22nd Century."

"Looking into 2167 with astonishment and wonder – using this ability of seeing which is not made of thought – we time travel into a dimension within our own selves and we envision optimal outcomes. The outermost planet of our solar system in Capricorn – the star sign constellation associated with time, structure, mathematics, society, cosmology, extra-terrestrials – prompts us to look into how time is actually structured.

"As voyagers of time we see this as a once every 250 years cycle of awareness, within a 26,000 year greater cycle, or one hundred times per cycle. When in rare aspects to Uranus and Saturn, as is the case in 2013 and 2047, it is a once every 2,000 years development, or 13 times per great cycle. With Neptune it is a one time only event.

"By 2020, unexamined beliefs are not worth holding unto. System managers and world leaders run into a serious identity crises because they are trying to hold on to archaic patterns of the mind, that in turn worship those obsolete structures of society we have to let go of.

"Belief systems, be they scientific or spiritual ones, see extreme changes with the discovery of the new noetic sciences – cosmology, artificial intelligence, orgone energy, new hemp applications, alternative medicine practiced by every human being, massive DNA breakthroughs, language communication, psychic perceptions, including breakthroughs in particle physics and molecular biology – that will transform all social structures on earth.

"There will be groundbreaking developments in *NewMind Technologies*, for disseminating all of these new realizations related to the invisible worlds as unique time capsules appear, and are discovered. This interview shows this trend, as it is appearing slightly ahead of its time. What is the key realization all about? *The advanced human mind-soul – in touch with the invisible worlds – is its own new technology.*

"This is a realization of immense scope, and it is also the discovery humanity has been evolving towards for the past twenty five thousand years. First of all we will address where we came from. A new history will be taught. All this will help to put mankind in its proper context. At the same time this will free mankind, one soul at a time."

Kerry paused to look at what seemed a very faint, almost ghostly light appearing against the stone wall at the opposite end of the great hall in *Chillon*. The subtle glow took the form of thousands of rainbow lights all concentrated in one mass. Appearing not to have seen this transient visitor, the Master of The Light continued to explain the dynamics of the future, as Kerry then asked unexpectedly:

"What is your role in the changes you outline here?"

91

"In ages past, I worked with Taoist time lords, an ancient order of advanced sages implementing the teachings of an inter-dimensional guidance from beyond time. I am here now to assist the development of a unified field and interstellar consciousness, by showing certain people how to re-invent and re-engineer themselves."

As he spoke these revealing words about his existence, the ghostly being of light faded into the ancient stones of the famous Templars castle walls.

"The work and its networks which I represent are not presented with *survival* in mind, but are concerned about living in and being part of this new development. As realities merge, and as the unseen force that has given rise to the physical, becomes visible to human beings by 2027, the invisible worlds become a more active part of the reality we create and live in.

"What would you advise people do in the decades ahead, knowing what you know?"

"In the timeless time ahead, we are well advised to move and be like water, to become Cosmic, to leave old thought structures, such as doubt, fear, secrecy and self-related quests behind. There is no system needed to let the mind soar. Where the soul is located there is no fear. Action without thought becomes possible, and this knowing is its own right action, in choiceless awareness.

"We are in a cycle in which we realize these fundamental things. A few at first, one by one, we begin to mutate to these facts of life. The discoveries initiated by our soul cover tens of thousands of years, reaching absolutely decisive momentum in the next forty years. We are moving into the eye of the needle of this issue in the next decade.

"Siberian sorcerers, as well as Templars' commanders and Taoist masters, taught their apprentices all these things. What is helpful is thoughtless thought, in total stillness, which is needed to move into unknown realms. Selflessness is helpful in order to better understand what we are discussing here. You may have your name and your position, and yet you are absolute nothingness.

"The new mind will no longer process information only in a linear manner. In fact linear thinking will be seen as a severe obstacle in the years to come. The evolved mind realizes, that to apply all this, it is necessary to be seeking and seeing in a selfless manner, without this false sense of the identity known as the self.

"Some of us will see and be taught by the Elves, and other inhabitants of many more dimensions than we thought possible. This is a process that will challenge humans to shift into a direct contact with their inner core intelligence. Thus, it is worth devoting some meditative moments to these discoveries. Eventually, scientists will explain all this in terms of mathematics and sacred geometry.

"Time travel begins to become common place – an occupation of time well spent. Voyagers from another reality have been – and are – in contact with the new minds emerging to share totally unknown realities, and to assist the process of the grand scale transformation of mankind.

"If you can apply this in your own life in some way, you are a very important key part of this new humanity, one that is about to emerge in the next two generations. What we discuss here cannot be managed, gained nor acquired in any manner, it can only be applied directly. Seeing is its own direct action, unrelated to any other process."

The stones of the castle rock echoed with his last words.

"This is the silent mind of the future."

"Having lived on earth for millennia, why are we as we are? What is the future of all of us? During that evolution of experience, knowledge in actual fact, what has happened to each of us? What shall we do if we see the fact that we are the entire humanity? What am I to do living in this corrupt society? Will whatever I do affect society? Am I different from society? Is there an action without motive, self-interest, or seeking gain that is not dependent on the past or a pattern of the future?"

~ Jiddu Krishnamurti

12
Codex From The Future

As the sun set below the Western mountain range, The Master of The Light quietly passed unnoticed, down the narrow stair well entrance to the granite bedrock foundations of *Chillon*. At the further end of the crystal chamber he disappeared into a vortex of light.

In December 2012, during the Mayan alignment, while at his hidden mountain installation in the Swiss Alps – in keeping with his ability to enter into any time zone of his choice – The Master of The Light accompanied Ta-Lor and her science team into 2137 – one hundred and thirty years from the date this initial report had been compiled.

2137 is the year when Neptune and Pluto form the rare opposition in line of fixed stars Antares and Aldebaran respectively. He entered the *installation* walls via the rainbow vortex, where he could view the holographic situation room in 2013. The information floated inside the crystal viewing screen as he studied the complex movements of the planets, and understood their influence on the humans on the planet down below.

Onto the screen advanced 2048, Pluto opposed Uranus in the same axis it did in the year 5 BC. *The Master of The Light* reminded the gathered time lords what 5 BC meant in the bigger picture of the aeon rotation. This exact alignment – from Pisces 9 to Virgo 9 – is in effect once every 2,000 years.

His intricate communications were complete concepts of telepathy. He began his silent explanation, giving an overview of the events in terms of planetary and cosmic dimensions.

Now, imagine that 2,000 years ago, a few timeless and guided wise ones in Aramea – call them sages or seers if you like – were holding interesting talks, kind of like *Krishnamurti* was doing during the last century in India, England, Switzerland or California. But the original or ancient

96

dialogues we are talking about here, were held in what is now known as the Middle East.

Krishnamurti gave talks that could be taped; both on audio and video, and he attracted a wide variety of people to him from all walks of life, some of who became seers and sages in their own right. Krishnamurti's teachings could not be altered and rewritten, he published his own talks into his own books. So, we have an advantage in this century to read, hear and see the original words, still carrying the original undiluted meaning.

Immanuel – better known as Jesus – gave talks, but his interactions with the people on earth were not recorded on video as he spoke, leaving space to later change and dilute his words and teachings. Now imagine that 2,000 years ago scribes were actually recording the talks of the sages as they spoke of highly unusual things such as the stars, the planets and deeper cosmology. They spoke about extra-terrestrials and the invisible worlds.

Scribes sat and scribbled the talks onto parchments and scrolls. But maybe they only actually wrote down what they heard, after the talks were given, with a fading memory of what was said, or with a systems error. Well, eventually the living memory of those talks got lost altogether.

Much later, even the writings themselves were lost, or made to disappear, even misused. Much later, the talks re-appear in altered fashion, having been rewritten, and we call these talks Scriptures. Older talks resurface and we call them Gnostic gospels, or even better codices.

We have with Pluto in time travel sign Capricorn the ultimate revelation of ancient wisdom: A collection of *Gnostic Files* from beyond the space-time continuum. In reality, what does it mean? This is the future scenario, shown in form of a high tech analogy – *Error 110101011 – Belief System Failure.*

The interesting thing about the Gospel phenomenon, and by extension all these other Gnostic re-discoveries – which is officially a Codex and not a Gospel, is that Judas was not part of the system of disinformation of the psychological operation known as religion.

The fragmentation of the true – the original – teachings of the sages, whether they came from India, Tibet or Atlantis, and what it really means, will be rectified through implementing a bridge of time from the original line into the future cultures of humans on earth.

The sages knew that their friends had no clue who they really were or where they really came from, since they had come to them from beyond the space time continuum.

Ta-Lor woke from a psychic review to consider that the masters of reality were teaching, not only that we came from the stars, but that the many forces around the earth were of extra-terrestrial origin, some of who were of the spiritually advanced kind from the future.

Those who understood the original teaching were overthrown through violence; their cultures and their knowledge were destroyed. There existed a basic truth that some control groups did not want passed from generation to generation.

The sages in Aramea signalled – The illusion is over. That was 2,000 years ago, as the age of Pisces dawned. In association with that phenomenon, the Draco, Reptilians and the Archontes or the Greys, began to rewire the hard drive interface of the human racial memory.

The anti-reality controllers, following the protocols of the dark lords, wound up messing around with the human DNA sequence. A fear-based Trojan Horse, mass mind control project, was implanted into the human genetics to make sure that the natural DNA configuration did not return to its original form, creating sovereign human beings. The error in the mind of man is what we call the ego.

The soul, which exists as a dynamic non physical quantum field, interfaces with your physical form in a similar way you interface with physical biological operating system. The creator of all that is, set up the original system within the DNA – much later the reptilians come along and hack into the system code; which is kind of what happened.

Here we are now 2,000 years later. We are approaching yet again the famous Pluto-Uranus alignment of 2,000 years ago. By 2048 we are within reach of the original light code.

A new aeon dawns in 2048, as the Pisces age of belief becomes the Aquarius age of knowing, with the water bearer pouring knowledge of Cosmos over this realm. This is a living medicine sign over the twelve astrological ages, known in the timeless Codex as aeons. Each one has its own awareness.

At each stage of your astrological development, over many life times known as levels of incarnations, your soul is clicking on files, some of them super-sensitive, and as you click around you are opening them up and working on them. You are akin to an internet connection into the real world web of life, allowing the soul to connect, communicate and interact with a hyper-reality.

This is what *QRC-2137* was perhaps all about. Someone or some thing, wants to disrupt the soul communication network, and so they spread their designer virus, they hack into the operating system. This makes it hard for us to use and develop the network given at sovereign birth.

The corrupted operating system is ego, the me, self importance. The virus is fear as time. Thought as experience creates the thinker. Study the Krishnamurti principle: *Thought and thinker are one.*

The 4th dimensional reptilians introduced a fear based *Trojan* into the operating system, in order to counteract the intelligence communications of the soul, which means you the ego answer back rather than carry out the required upgrade as part of your own soul development.

As we grow through life times of incarnation levels, the soul clicks on files that will expand and enhance our development, resonating with the source to carry out the necessary tasks. Reading a codex from the future, or a mind altering book is a life of soul enhancement.

Living in nature creates a resonant file of enhancement, as is planting and eating the right food, healing and protecting the earth, developing new ways to interact with the environment, humanly and energetically engineered nutrition, developing an advanced economy, while moving between the worlds – enhancing a soul

All of these sane things are soul enhancing files stored in the DNA operating system of mankind. But due to the ego, which is time and fear-based, when the soul enhancing files get clicked open, *thought* opposes intelligence, wishing to design its own operating system.

The problem is that we run thoughts non stop through the brain until thoughts run amok, go off on tangents and take over the whole brain, reconnecting nerve pathways. This is HAL-9000 in Kubrick's *2001 – A Space-Odyssey*, where intelligence steps in and eventually disconnects thought, the out of control machine.

One must *stop* and press *pause*! Where are the thoughts coming from? Observe! Pay attention! What is the deeper pattern? The inner awareness has to stay centered no matter what is coming into the mind from outside. When we sit still, we create silence in the mind, through observation. The inner intelligence is peace of mind.

All this super reactive behaviour comes from thought, which is time and fear-based, the ego interfering with the original design, and this type of interference divides our existence on earth from *first soul contact*. All religions, and all political and scientific belief systems take the human earth child and bombard it with fear-based systems. These systems of psychological fear are there to activate the damaged hard drive, to suppress the original cosmic operating system.

The human race has been hijacked and its journey delayed, which is where it stands now. Connection to First Source is only possible from within, and not via the manuals known as *scriptures*.

The Master of The Light merged with the holographic field, showing scenes from the altered history of mankind. He walked straight into the newly built temples of ancient Greece. No one on the screen appeared to see him, as he moved behind the scenes of the ancient Parthenon temples, and out into the sunlight.

The scenes changed into Judea. People were running carelessly through the narrow dusty streets, fleeing the Roman centurions, just as two millennia later we would see the Buddhist monks fleeing the Chinese soldiers running through the streets in Burma.

He appeared in Paris, as the Moon, Saturn, Uranus and Neptune aligned in the 12th degree of Scorpio. It was the 30th of September 1307, two weeks before the Knights Templars were arrested by Phillip the Fair. The Templars commander asked The Master of The Light to take their treasure into safety. He carried their secrets into the future.

The holograph seemed to fade. The Master of The Light passed through the vortex portal where he appeared to walk between fragile cracks of rainbow light.

Ta-Lor opened the super computer no one had ever operated before, and entered the required commands via a new crystal slate technology, using very ancient *Tai Chi* and *Tao Te Ch'ing* techniques to operate a holographic force field. The spiral arrow sign appeared on the screen.

Onto the crystal slate comes *First Contact*, known by now as the future database *QRC-2137 – The Codex from the Future*, and we started all over again.

The solar eclipse moved over the cursor on her small crystal slate screen, while Ta-Lor activated it with one click on her wrist watch – to see writings of Jiddu Krishnamurti appear within the holographic light source. She read:

"Thought and the thinker are one, but it is thought that creates the thinker, and without thought there is no thinker. So one has to be aware of the process of conditioning, which is thought; and when there is awareness of that process without choice, when there is no sense of resistance, when there is neither condemnation nor justification of what is observed, then we see that the mind is the centre of conflict.

"In understanding the mind and the ways of the mind, the conscious as well as the unconscious, through dreams, through every word, through every process of thought and action, the mind becomes extraordinarily quiet; and that tranquillity of the mind is the beginning of wisdom.

Wisdom cannot be bought, it cannot be learnt; it comes into being only when the mind is quiet, utterly still—not made still by compulsion, coercion, or discipline. Only when the mind is spontaneously silent is it possible to understand that which is beyond time."

13
The 13th Consciousness

13 October 2007 – In heliocentric terms, the earth and the moon were conjunct in the 20th degree of Aries. Mercury had begun its retrograde motion in Scorpio, and the moon mirrored exactly the alignment of September 30, 1307.

Seven hundred years after the arrest of the Templars, The Master of The Light touches the crown of his watch to bring up the crystal screen of his *SpaceStar* timepiece. It is a bright autumn day; on the screen he observes a woman carefully lift an old weathered scroll from the shelves of the Vatican Secret Archive; she is holding the *Chinon parchment*. The document exonerates the Templars, absolving them of the Vatican's false accusations against their order.

The *Chinon parchment* explains, in detail, how the pope is obliged to ask the Templars for pardon for his crimes against mankind. On October 25th, 2007, the Vatican published the book of the trial proceedings against the Templars, once more falsifying the context of the murders.

Professor Barbara Frale, researching the Secret Archives of The Vatican in Rome, housing the stolen wisdom of the ancient world, opened the *Chinon parchment*. The Vatican could no longer delay the release of crucial source documents relating to the disappearance of the monks who had activated and financed the meta-consciousness when they were massacred in Paris.

"This is proof that the Templars were not heretics," said Professor Frale. "The Pope was obliged to ask pardon from the knights."

Why had the Templars been arrested? This question had preoccupied the world for seven long centuries. The French monarchy reacted to the power of the monks by triggering a true blackmail mechanism, which urged Pope Clement V to reach the ambiguous compromise ratified during the Council of Vienne in 1312.

Unable to oppose the will of the King of France, Phillip the Fair, who imposed the elimination of the Templars, the pope removed the Templar Order from the reality of that period, without condemning or abolishing it, but isolating it in a hibernation for seven hundred years, thus deleting the wisdom carriers of Cosmos from the collective memory. The Master of The Light reinstated this memory into the consciousness of mankind when Jupiter passed in line of Pluto over the Galactic Center, in December 2007.

The relevance of the document cannot be understood in terms of the faked *trial proceedings* of 1313, which took place to hide the real intention of abolishing *The 13th Consciousness*, as taught by The Master of The Light in *The Atlantis Oracle*.

On November 3rd 2013, during the annular total eclipse, in the 12th degree of Scorpio, with master of time Saturn in Scorpio – in line of the *Southern Cross Constellation* – a young Nepalese woman picks up a smooth, clear crystal tablet. The disk shaped plate activates at the touch of her hands, the crystal comes aglow with an indigo blue light. Reading from the crystal's surface, the powerful hieroglyphs communicate their eternal meaning in her own language. The Master of The Light stands with his back to the magnificent Nepalese mountains watching the young woman read the tablet of the ancient voyagers of time. The light-encoded words came alive:

… Eons before our recorded time, long before sacred and secret knowledge was passed on by word of mouth, hand signs, or written symbols, a civilization existed that evidenced the likely presence of super-human intelligence, more advanced than yours will be even in centuries to come. Seeded by star beings, this land known as *Atlantis* flourished somewhere in space-time before the last Ice Age.

The great occultists of that ancient, lost, and sunken world of Atlantis are believed to have crafted the Zodiac system that forms the basis of the *art of astrology*, the science of ancient civilizations from outer space. The creation of the Zodiac goes back far enough in time to a period when the origin of its signs and symbols coincided exactly with the respective constellation positions in the heavens. Scholars consequently estimate the Zodiac was invented five million years ago, during a time beyond time.

The star travellers of Atlantis – voyagers of time – created symbolic creatures to illustrate the *meaning* of the Zodiac. They invented legends and myths to help us understand and remember the symbolic content. They also incorporated the zodiacal system into symbols and projection holders known later as Tarot cards as an additional method of divining and understanding human nature.

They knew that when a spirit descended into material existence, it incarnated through one of the twelve signs of the Zodiac, each ruled by a particular planet, or wanderer, as they called those heavenly bodies that were not fixed, as for instance, the bright star Sirius, or the constellation of Orion, the hunter. They had a complete understanding of each of the two hundred fixed star's energy and meaning.

The Divine Order of a celestial hierarchy did exist once upon a time. The law of analogy – as above so below – is a wise teaching bequeathed to us by the ancient voyagers of Atlantis who had a remarkable understanding of humankind and Cosmos. They took the concept that man is made in the image of Creation as literal alchemy.

They maintained that the universe was an organism not unlike the human body, and every phase and function of the *Universal Body* has its correspondence in man. Therefore, to the wise stargazers, the study of the stars and astrological alignments was a sacred art, a secret science, and serious business. They were seers with total psychic recall and a complete understanding of destiny. They knew that the overall geometry of alignments reflected the medical and energetic health of a civilization.

The Atlantean wise men and women saw in the movements of the heavenly bodies the ever present activity of the great Architect of the Universe. Among others, their descendants, the Pythagoreans, were often criticized by an ignorant world for promulgating doctrines of metempsychosis, transmigration of the souls. Those mystics, like the Atlanteans, believed the spiritual nature of man descended into material existence from the *Milky Way*, the seed ground of the souls, through one of the twelve signs of the Zodiacal band of stars. In fact they assigned twenty-two gates for the arrival of a soul on earth.

The seers of Atlantis viewed creation as being in various stages of becoming. Sand grains eventually became human consciousness; human beings became planets, which in turn became solar systems and then cosmic chains, on and on, ad infinitum.

The Zodiac belt was one stage of development between the solar system and the cosmic chain. Master stargazers, thinkers, and creators of astrological systems, the Atlanteans possessed knowledge that eventually became the basis for ancient Heliocentric and Ptolemaic – or geocentric – views of the universe and of the Egyptian, Babylonian, and Assyrian science of astrology.

In the beginning, the extra-terrestrials divided the Cosmos among themselves, proportionate according to their respective dignities. Each one of their representatives became the peculiar carrier of his or her own allotment, establishing sacred spaces and ordaining a seer craft, which instituted a system of knowing.

To the planet Neptune was given the sea and a vast island continent in the midst of it. Three earth born humans lived on a mountaintop in the middle of that giant island: Evenor, his wife, Leucipe, and their lovely daughter, Cleito. After the sudden death of her parents, Poseidon took the girl under his wings. She eventually bore him ten sons. Poseidon then subdivided the continent into ten states and made his eldest son, Atlas, overlord above the other nine. He named his continent Atlantis, after his eldest son, and he called the sea surrounding it, the Atlantic.

The descendants of Atlas continued their benign rule over Atlantis during countless generations. With wise industry and efficient government, they elevated the continent to unsurpassed dignity. Natural resources were limitless, ores were mined, quarries were managed, wild animals were domesticated, and science, arts, and crafts were perfected and practiced. Throughout this time, no wars were ever fought. Peace was the operating principle of this civilization.

While enjoying the natural abundance of their semi-tropic location, Atlantean architects planned and erected stunning palaces, temples, pyramids, docks, tunnels and bridges creating canals and central islands. The citadel in the center was a sanctuary of bliss surrounded by a wall of solid gold. The City of the Golden Gates – *Numenor* – and capital of Atlantis had a tower reaching into the stratospheres.

Poseidon's temple, made of silver, gold, and ivory, contained a colossal statue of Poseidon standing in a chariot drawn by half a dozen winged horses surrounded by a hundred graceful Nereids playing on dolphins. This temple was a space portal for the voyagers of time coming in from planet Neptune. There were hot and cold springs, meditation retreats, and to the great harbor came vessels from the other maritime nations. Vast plains yielded two crops a year...

The young woman in Nepal briefly looked to the snow-covered peaks of the timeless mountains, holding the crystal tablet as if it was something sacred. Her eyes were alight with the wisdom from the stars. She once more gazed into the crystal.

...Every year the ten kings of Atlantis would meet; donning their azure or golden robes, passing sentences while sitting in judgment, taking a renewed oath of loyalty upon a sacred inscription. Their chief law stated that they would never take up arms against each other and they would assist each other in the event someone from the outside world attacked one of them. No king had power of life and death over his kinsmen without a majority approval among the ten kings' council of Atlantis. They operated in concert with an extra-terrestrial council of Cosmos.

Filled with false ambitions and lured from the pathway of wisdom and virtue by evil temptations, the rulers of Atlantis decided one day to conquer the rest of the world. That was the beginning of the end of their glory and their history.

In 9600 B.C. Jupiter gathered his armies and told them he would not permit this warlike behaviour of the Atlanteans to continue. Violent earthquakes and deluge-like floods occurred. As a result, Atlantis sank beneath the sea and disappeared, never to be seen again. This is how the story is told. The truth is that the seers had to disconnect Atlantis from an impending attack by the hostile alien presence.

Partly historical and partly allegorical, the description of Atlantis conceals profound philosophical mysteries. If the sinking of the island continent of Atlantis is viewed from the realm of the archetypal, then its complete submersion into the sea is seen as the descent of rational, intuitive intelligence, harmonized with *Universal Order*, into the chaotic divided delusion of mortal ignorance.

As the mother of all metaphors, Atlantis, as an allegory, brings to mind the archetypal images of the fall of man from a divine to a mortal state. However, Atlantis most likely dates back aeons before these scriptural allusions, as confirmed by modern geological, archaeological, and zoological findings that keep showing up. Yet the story of Atlantis is similar to the misunderstood account of the fall of man into the temptations of knowledge, signifying spiritual involution, as a prerequisite to conscious evolution. How can we know and choose the good if we haven't tested and tasted evil?

The esoteric and scientific knowledge of the Atlantis seer craft survived, but in fragments. Either via trade or cross-cultural exchanges of those times, the wisdom of Atlantis spread to other parts of the world. According to legend, when the spiritually illumined initiates, wise men, and seers of Atlantis realized their land was coming under the control of dark magicians who had left the path of light, they fled to Egypt, South America, India, Nepal, and Scotland. They took with them their symbols along with their secret doctrines for the purpose of training and educating new civilizations in Cosmic science.

In the midst of the Atlantean program of planned world colonization and conversion, gigantic cataclysms sank their homeland. The Atlantean initiate seers, who had promised to come back to their settlements, never returned; and after the lapse of millennia, tradition preserved fragments of a fantastic account of gods who came from a place where now there is only the sea.

South American, as well as other cultures, such as those of Brittany and Tibet, or the American Indians and Nepalese, contain remnants of a great and lost civilization similar to Atlantis. No one knows with certainty about Atlantis. A single great mystery remains that has its origin in an era long past.

It sheds light on Atlantis via its inherent scientific link: The Sphinx and its many tetrahedron pyramids on the Giza plateau in Egypt – reduced versions of the originals on Mars and Sirius – are time portals used by extra-terrestrials as communication centers for their interstellar journeys. It has now been geologically proven that the Sphinx is older than the last Ice Age and that there lies, hidden from view, a deep cavern or empty space beneath the front paws of the lion. A black, disk-shaped star ship is concealed in that space and will be discovered by 2020.

Apart from the fabled image of feathered men who came from the seas or the skies, also known as UFOs, the mythology of all humanity contains reminders of the Atlantean Golden Age, the transcendence of their great wisdom and the sanctity of their main symbols, the cross and serpent along with the skull and bones.

That they actually had come in space vessels was soon forgotten, for untutored minds considered even such primitive boats, as the one Columbus sailed when he set foot on the Bahamas, as super-natural. It is not hard to imagine the effect of an aircraft would have on people from a technologically unsophisticated society.

The hidden Akashic records will be found and explained by the time Neptune is in Pisces, around 2020. Atlantis was, is, and always will be the single most unresolved mystery of human history. Where was it, where did it come from, and where did it go? What is it all about? All we had until now were sources, such as the ancient Greek philosopher Plato or the historian Herodotus, who said: *Man's fortune never abides in the same place.*

According to these sources, the Atlanteans lived Aeons before the ancient Egyptian civilizations that built the Sphinx and great pyramids – all lined up to mirror the Dog Star Sirius and the constellation of Orion. Geologists have proven, beyond reasonable doubt, that the Sphinx is at least twelve millennia old; hence, the lion's body, since it was built in the Age of Leo. Explorers making other discoveries linked to Atlantis in the Puerto Rico Trench, the Bermuda Triangle, around Bimini Island in the Bahamas, off Cuba, and near the Azores, say they found traces of Atlantis below the pole caps. Nepal will reveal the transcript of its Atlantean consciousness.

Atlantis existed long before the Sphinx. It mysteriously sunk below the surface of the earth and became known as the *Lost Continent*, after which other civilizations, linked closer to us in historical time, took over by bringing remnants of Atlantean esoteric knowledge to us.

There were myriad movements – Mayan, Incan, Celtic Druidic, Nordic, Hindu, Shamanic, Shaolin, Sufi, Zen, Tibetan, Chaldean, Babylonian, Assyrian, Aramaic, Egyptian, Greek, Roman, Hebrew, Essenes, Hyperborean – along with other such schools of thought and secret societies as the Knights Templars and Pythagoreans. Much of the true knowledge is hidden in the Vatican City's Secret Archives.

The adventurous spirit of humankind, seeking knowledge and the stars, was carried into the Aquarian Age by men in golden suits who landed on the moon and by the launching of instruments for observation, exploration, and discovery – such as *Voyager 11*, and out into the far reaches of the solar system, far beyond the orbits of Neptune, or even Pluto's spheres. We are emerging from Kali Yuga and recapturing some of the glory that was Atlantis.

Yesterday is gone. We can learn from it and try not to repeat its mistakes. Tomorrow is yet to come. We can control its manifestation only by the choices we make in the present moment. The now is what counts, what we can shape, influence, and transform. Consider this as you interact with any system of High Magic, be it the Viking Runes, the Chinese I Ching, the Tarot, or the knowing of astrological alignments in motion, past, present, and future.

Realize that you will foresee events and perhaps sequences of circumstances, people, or places. However, you will not see actual timelines or any distinction between past present, and future. It will not happen because time is only an illusion, however persistent. A true seer understands that it is impossible to foretell the future, because all that can be foreseen are screenplays of possibilities.

The concept of time is a creation and illusion of the human mind, based on thought, because thought is time. It is an attempt to structure manifestations in the material dimension. It is a by-product of the collective subconscious prison of human experience, from which we would now free ourselves. Time is non-existent to the *Cosmic Mind* and irrelevant to the human mind that is in tune with Spirit.

In order to be open to the light and knowledge of the Aquarian Age, we must relearn much of what we previously thought to be true, including our concept of space-time. We must remember what was once known.

A few pictures are worth millions of words regarding the human psyche or its origins on planet Earth. The pictograms, archetypes, symbols and dreams are travels of the soul that have been recorded in one form or another ever since reptiles started walking on two legs as was told in the sagas about the men from the seas.

Caves filled with mysterious petroglyphs, tombs of secrets built all over this planet, show us what kind of fears and hopes preoccupied our ancestors; and might they be the wise druids and savant sages flown in from other galaxies? Was Atlantis constructed by, or with the aid of, high-tech space beings, or was it a magnificent story written by Plato – a hallucinatory initiation dream originating within an Egyptian pyramid? Now you know the answer.

Surrounded by the beauty of Nepal, the young woman absorbed the notions from the crytal slate...

We, the Atlantean seers who left you this crystal tablet from beyond time came from the stars. We are your future. The people who populated the civilization of Atlantis had an intelligence far greater than yours. Atlantis was founded by beings from other star systems. The mystery of the building of Atlantis is similar to the uncertainty concerning the origins of the Zodiac. We have proof in the form of symbols, signs, and glyphs recorded as divination systems in ancient Egypt, all of which are reminiscent of *Atlantean Oracles*. We know that the symbols used by our seers were given to them by an extra-terrestrial intelligence of high cultures, and ultimately they were of Cosmic origin.

You may ask this: Is human history pre-destined? If it is predictable, do we have the freedom to change or effect the outcome? Enlightened scholars and philosophers of all ages have attempted to discover answers to these questions. Seeking illumination throughout time in the study of recorded mythology; ancient scriptures, tablets, scrolls and books, they found no answer.

Some fear based intolerant belief systems, designed to control the human mind, teach that it is blasphemous or satanic to predict and change the future, to delve into mysteries such as life after death and re-incarnation, to consider lives we may or may not have lived before this present one, or the lives we will live in the future.

Now you know that you must know the answer to these questions. The answer is written in the stars...

14
Guidance Revealed

The blue Atlantic Ocean crashed onto the sandy shore outside the austere home of the master astrologer. In the distance an opaque haze shimmered above the Bimini Islands, giving an almost supra-natural mirage-like presence to the Bermuda Triangle. The sun rise on the last day of February reflected golden light into his eyes, as The Master of The Light walked silently into the study commanding a breathtaking view over the endless sea.

The astrologer looked up from his ephemeris. He turned to gaze around his living space, sensing a presence observing his efforts to put his calculated visions into words. The small white cat with the black tail suddenly jumped onto her friend's table, touching the keyboard with her paw, seeking attention. She stared intently at The Master of The Light, as he watched his own incarnation at work. The time lord was close to completing the last stage of his *Atlantean Oracle*, while the moon moved into the 13th degree of Scorpio.

Pluto opposed the sun, shining brightly over the ocean in the 9th degree of Pisces. Jupiter in line of Antares opposed Mars. The four planets formed a square across the heavens, a perfect cross in the four mutable signs – Mars in line of fixed star *Aldebaran*, known to the Ancients as the star of the seers, in *Arachne, the 13th sign*. He studied the mysterious birth chart he knew by heart; twenty-four more hours left until leap day – a marker of his own choice. He smiled knowingly at the little cat, as he designed his noetic star science.

... In the Middle Ages, the world was understood according to a metaphor based on Dante's allegorical Inferno, *Purgatorio*, and *Paradiso*, of nine concentric spheres that included seven planets and the fixed stars. Life on earth was seen as mirroring arrangements believed to exist in the heavens where everything had its fixed place.

Tomorrow was as solid and predictable as the knowledge of yesterday. Today was just one more link in the chain of cause and effect in a Divine scheme of things with man on planet Earth sitting safely in the center of creation.

Things remained safe for another few centuries. Cosmos was a gigantic galactic clock, wound by the Creator. We found the ultimate analogy – known as *the clock of destiny*. Cosmos was set in motion and was completely understandable through the eyes of the great mathematician, a perfectly mechanical world, or so it seemed for a while. Egyptian hermetic science seemed to confirm this.

Quantum physics told us what the world is not, but as we swept away those layers, what eventually was left became more and more bizarre until we realized we also had discarded the reason and logic that was the foundation of our former world views. What remained before our eyes was no more comprehensible via logic than the readings of the Runes and chicken entrails we had so happily abandoned in a search for scientific truth. We returned to High Magic and the power of the human mind.

How solid Newton's clock seemed with its eternal ticking in which time and objects in space had a definite past and an assured future; the behaviour of Cosmos seemed to obey solid laws of matter. However, the clock metaphor had broken its spring, and the assurance it once provided evaporated with Heisenberg's famous *Uncertainty Principle*, which denies us the concrete knowledge of a particle's position *and* momentum.

In our infinite cleverness, we had assumed that a particle's attributes were definite set values, and that the process of measurement disturbed the particles to the point that the measured attributes were changed by our measuring. This disturbance model of measurement was briefly thought to account for all the quirky results physicists were producing, such as quantum randomness and Heisenberg's uncertainty relations.

Since particles are the building blocks of everything in Cosmos, there is a necessary link between the behaviour of these minuscule units and the objects composed of them, including our minds and ourselves. In a curious twist of the inexplicable link between all things, experimenters searching within the brain's structure for a physical foundation for the concepts of the thinking mind, and for the 13th consciousness, discovered that the brain contains structures called micro-tubules. These substances contain an electron held in the same indeterminate state as the particles that make up everything else in Cosmos.

Furthermore, the position of this electron in the micro-tubule cavity determines the protein composition of the molecule and the function of the micro-tubule. Here is the curious fact: If the electron is paralyzed within the micro-tubule, when a gaseous anaesthetic is used on a human being, that person loses consciousness. From this bit of data, experimenters extrapolated the *theory* that it is the moving electron in the micro-tubule that gives rise to the absolute or 13th consciousness, and to the thinking mind. At this point, we enter unknown territory. If the conscious mind indeed is the result of a quantum process, or the indeterminate electron in the micro-tubule, and our whole perception of reality is a function of the mind, then that perception is ultimately grounded in the quantum process, with its quirky behaviour.

How does this information affect our experience of events around us? When considering the past, for example, could it be that what we perceive as the present is brought about by an act of mind functioning through a quantum process, creating experience by collapsing the many possible options before us into one determinate event?

In that case, what comprises the future? Could our ideas of the future merely be our intimation of the possible states of experience held in their potential form within our minds? Could it actually be, as we are told, that if we visualize success with some endeavour, we actually create the reality we so desire?

What significance does the above inference have within the framework of divination from oracles? Could it be that, at a subconscious level, we pick the most likely array of Tarot cards or Runes from all the possible choices – the one that most closely corresponds to the reality we are in the process of creating? The question is fascinating.

Using the old mind, we cannot positively answer this, anymore than today's scientists can answer questions arising from the mystifying quantum process. But, we can ask our 13th consciousness – using *NewMind Technologies* – how to imagine the solution.

Although we must live with the mysteries of the future, we become more aware of the role the mind plays in effecting our choices and experiences. If we can predict forthcoming events via star science and astrology, *and* change our thoughts, then we are masters of destiny who transform not only ourselves, but also our future worlds. We will not discover our future, we create it. Ahead of us lies a new and supra-natural reality.

…And the golden face of the Buddha smiled across the ending of time.

Emperor Wu of China – a most benevolent Buddhist – had built many temples and monasteries, educated many monks, and performed countless philanthropic deeds in the name of the great Buddha.

And so, one day, he the great Emperor Wu of China asked the great teacher Bodhidharma: "What merit is there in my good works?"

Bodhidharma replied: "None whatsoever."

The Emperor then asked: "What is the Primal Meaning of Holy Reality?"

Bodhidharma answered: "Emptiness, not holiness."

The Emperor then queried: "Who, then, is this man confronting me?"

"I do not know," was Bodhidharma's reply.

Since the Emperor did not understand, Bodhidharma left his kingdom.

Later, Emperor Wu related this conversation to his trusted and confidential adviser, Prince Shiko, who reprimanded him, saying that Bodhidharma was the wisest and greatest teacher of all times in the realm – and possessed of the highest truth.

The Emperor, filled with deepest sorrow, sadness and heartfelt regret, dispatched a top secret messenger to entreat the wise sage to return. But Prince Shiko warned:

"Even if all the people in the land went, that one will never return. Never again."

15
The Way Home

In 2013, shortly after our last *Château Chillon* meeting, *The Master of The Light* signalled to me that we were ready to shift beyond the current phase, nine hundred years into the future of our Third Millennium, and move into the new time travel continuum where his *QRC-2137 project teams* were now fully operational.

When I asked him how we would leave this place, a white magnetically levitated space shuttle, with the group's spiral arrow markings on its tail fin, appeared in a reality window close to the lake. Our rendezvous was the 13th moon. I would observe the moment when the mother ship – a huge craft – ejected dozens of jet-like space shuttles, all sailing quietly into the night air within the earth field.

The beautiful sleek shuttle, made of titanium and gold, stood on tarmac one, shining brightly. The outer field of the elegant craft began gleaming blue, then silvery white. On top, in its doorway, stood the Master of The Light – observing the surrounding landscape.

The journey to the orbiter was short. Minutes later we docked with the space station, where our team was transferred to the black disk-shaped *Nordic* craft. The vessel was a work of engineering art beyond description.

The Master of The Light was greeted by one of his *Nordic* friends, whom I recognized from ages ago, and yet we were now in a time line that resembled 2913. The Nordics explained that they had disconnected all hostile forces. The space weaponization program had been annulled.

The navigation engineer handed me a compact crystal slate. I activated it by my awareness, and through it I saw a clear picture of the earth floating in an endless quantum sea of space. As we shifted into the future the earth itself looked pure and pristine. Forests stretched from seashores to mountain ranges. There were no cities, and no ships crossing the oceans.

It was as though no human being had altered the purity of the planet below. The earth appeared lush and clean, a blue gem sparkling in the depths of space. The ice caps had melted. I remembered the sight from when we had first landed here 26,000 years ago. I asked my old friend why the crystal showed no sign of human life on planet Earth?

He smiled and stated, "Cosmos erased the old memory, deleting the anti-reality. The hostile presence is gone. Soon we will be landing on our new home star base. Enjoy the voyage!"

NewMind Technologies made it possible to start anew, with highly advanced beings. Inherent to their vast knowledge is their gentle behaviour – a genuine friendliness. An ancient Nordic *Being of Knowing* steered the aware star craft with its mind – floating in the cockpit while communicating the knowledge we required to adapt to our destination.

This super being was neither masculine nor feminine. We were conscious of the fact that it was omnipresent, integrated into our destiny, like some sort of living data bank filled with distant compassion. This prescient being knew our future and our past. If I had to design God, this being would have been it.

The Master of The Light sat in an ergonomically engineered seer navigation field. The mother of pearl display case clicked open on his *SpaceStar* wrist watch. He activated the built in astrological ephemeris, studying with focus and intent the positions of planets and star sign constellations for the next two thousand years; something he loved to do in meditative trance when he had nothing more pressing to attend to.

He leaned back and swivelled his seat around to face me, as I studied the crystal holograph, gazing out into deep dark space. Together, we saw the stars fly by at what must have been a speed of about one quantum second per solar system.

Our craft soon came to a gigantic blue nebula, its size beyond all imagination, a living awareness hovering in deep space like a deep pool of water awaiting our return. The presence of the powerful being emanated from this blue nebula. As we entered the outer edges of the field we instantly understood the totality of our integrated existence.

These wise and powerful beings were ourselves, far advanced, in the future. They had led and guided us from times beyond time. We understood their purpose and design. While the purpose was elusive, its design was evidently to self-create, and in doing so become part of *Cosmic Awareness* – beyond time and space.

*   *   *

The Teaching

"The ending of thought frees your energetic body to resonate with the time travel continuum. Connect with yourself – and others – from the future, expanding your intuitive intelligence across the bridge of time. In the moment you see that you come from a long and timeless lineage of perennial teachers who represent a balanced inter-planetary culture, you instantly tap into your inner navigational guidance. You are the chief Architect of your own existence over many incarnations – vibrating within the presence of a living force beyond time."

~ St.Clair

January 31, 2137 – Neptune at 8 degrees Sagittarius in line of Antares, did oppose – as planned – Pluto at 8 degrees Gemini in line of Aldebaran, known as the Atlantean star of the seers. This superb and once in ten thousand years alignment was foreseen as the manifestation of a *Hyper-Dimensional Reality Zone* – interpreted as *The Force Field*. The new *meta-concept* was in sight, yet out of reach; and by knowing that we came from our own future – and from the stars – we unified our species into a cohesive creative design. This is the core message of the gentle being from the future who visited Earth when Jupiter aligned with Pluto in the Galactic Centre – with a powerful shared vision of hope.

Bigger – Better & More Beautiful

"The Man with The Golden Face had a fantastic vision of a tiny and faraway star with evolved beings. They used no technology to do things. They took life seriously, remaining close to home. They may have owned the finest space crafts in Cosmos, and yet they never went places. They may have controlled an advanced stealth beam weaponry, but kept it locked up – securely hidden.

They had few responsibilities; they never had to refer to a check list to remember what to do. They enjoyed A Simple Life – functional homes and healthy foods. They lived modestly yet comfortably, while keeping their traditions alive. They had no interest in leaving their planets where they grew old in peace – to pass on to other worlds with lives well lived."

~ The St.Clair Tao

$$2007$$

$$2008 \qquad 2009$$

$$2010 \qquad\qquad 2011$$

$$2012 \qquad 2013 \qquad 2014$$

$$2015 \qquad\qquad 2016$$

$$2017 \qquad 2018$$

$$2019$$

Time capsule contains calculations
by The Master of The Light

The five outer planets – Jupiter, Saturn, Uranus, Neptune and Pluto, plus Chiron – are positioned in the following degrees and star signs on January 1st of each year. Understanding the 360 Sabian symbols of the Zodiac compass shows you what the years ahead entail, when applied to planet positions.

Seeing the following list awakens a feeling for the global mood and pace. Knowing your birth chart helps to position you in the Zeitgeist or motions of times yet to come. Geometric aspects formed between planets are keys to reading past, present, and future of mankind – on and off earth. Keep this capsule safe!

Astrological Ephemeris
2008-2183

"Deep in the human unconscious is a pervasive need for a logical universe that makes sense. But the real universe is always one step beyond logic."

~ Frank Herbert, *Dune*

1.1.2008:
Jupiter 4 Capricorn, Saturn 9 Virgo,
Uranus 16 Pisces, Neptune 21 Aquarius,
Pluto 30 Sagittarius, Chiron 14 Aquarius

1.1.2009:
Jupiter 29 Capricorn, Saturn 22 Virgo,
Uranus 20 Pisces, Neptune 23 Aquarius,
Pluto 2 Capricorn, Chiron 19 Aquarius

1.1.2010:
Jupiter 27 Aquarius, Saturn 5 Libra,
Uranus 24 Pisces, Neptune 25 Aquarius,
Pluto 4 Capricorn, Chiron 24 Aquarius

1.1.2011:
Jupiter 27 Pisces, Saturn 17 Libra,
Uranus 27 Pisces, Neptune 27 Aquarius,
Pluto 6 Capricorn, Chiron 28 Aquarius

1.1.2012:
Jupiter 1 Taurus, Saturn 29 Libra,
Uranus 1 Aries, Neptune 29 Aquarius,
Pluto 8 Capricorn, Chiron 2 Pisces

1.1.2013:
Jupiter 8 Gemini, Saturn 10 Scorpio,
Uranus 5 Aries, Neptune 2 Pisces,
Pluto 10 Capricorn, Chiron 7 Pisces

1.1.2014:
Jupiter 17 Cancer, Saturn 21 Scorpio,
Uranus 9 Aries, Neptune 4 Pisces,
Pluto 13 Capricorn, Chiron 10 Pisces

1.1.2015:
Jupiter 22 Leo, Saturn 1 Sagittarius,
Uranus, 13 Aries, Neptune 6 Pisces,
Pluto 14 Capricorn, Chiron 14 Pisces

1.1.2016:
Jupiter 24 Virgo, Saturn 12 Sagittarius,
Uranus 17 Aries, Neptune 8 Pisces,
Pluto 16 Capricorn, Chiron 18 Pisces

1.1.2017:
Jupiter 22 Libra, Saturn 22 Sagittarius,
Uranus 21 Aries, Neptune 10 Pisces,
Pluto 17 Capricorn, Chiron 22 Pisces

1.1.2018:
Jupiter 17 Scorpio, Saturn 2 Capricorn,
Uranus 25 Aries, Neptune 12 Pisces,
Pluto 19 Capricorn, Chiron 25 Pisces

1.1.2019:
Jupiter 12 Sagittarius, Saturn 12 Capricorn,
Uranus 29 Aries, Neptune 15 Pisces,
Pluto 21 Capricorn, Chiron 29 Pisces

1.1.2020:
Jupiter 7 Capricorn, Saturn 22 Capricorn,
Uranus 3 Taurus, Neptune 17 Pisces,
Pluto 23 Capricorn, Chiron 2 Aries

1.1.2021:
Jupiter 3 Aquarius, Saturn 2 Aquarius,
Uranus 7 Taurus, Neptune 19 Pisces,
Pluto 25 Capricorn, Chiron 6 Aries

1.1.2022:
Jupiter 1 Pisces, Saturn 12 Aquarius,
Uranus 11 Taurus, Neptune 21 Pisces,
Pluto 26 Capricorn, Chiron 9 Aries

1.1.2023:
Jupiter 2 Aries, Saturn 23 Aquarius,
Uranus 16 Taurus, Neptune 23 Pisces,
Pluto 28 Capricorn, Chiron 12 Aries

1.1.2024:
Jupiter 6 Taurus, Saturn 4 Pisces,
Uranus 20 Taurus, Neptune 26 Pisces,
Pluto 30 Capricorn, Chiron 16 Aries

1.1.2025:
Jupiter 14 Gemini, Saturn 15 Pisces,
Uranus 24 Taurus, Neptune 28 Pisces,
Pluto 2 Aquarius, Chiron 20 Aries

1.1.2026:
Jupiter 22 Cancer, Saturn 27 Pisces,
Uranus 28 Taurus, Neptune 30 Pisces,
Pluto 3 Aquarius, Chiron 23 Aries

1.1.2027:
Jupiter 27 Leo, Saturn 9 Aries,
Uranus 3 Gemini, Neptune 2 Aries,
Pluto 5 Aquarius, Chiron 27 Aries

1.1.2028:
Jupiter 28 Virgo, Saturn 22 Aries,
Uranus 7 Gemini, Neptune 4 Aries,
Pluto 6 Aquarius, Chiron 1 Taurus

1.1.2029:
Jupiter 25 Libra, Saturn 5 Taurus,
Uranus 12 Gemini, Neptune 7 Aries,
Pluto 8 Aquarius, Chiron 4 Taurus

1.1.2030:

Jupiter 21 Scorpio, Saturn 19 Taurus,
Uranus 16 Gemini, Neptune 9 Aries,
Pluto 10 Aquarius, Chiron 9 Taurus

1.1.2031:
Jupiter 16 Sagittarius, Saturn 3 Gemini,
Uranus 21 Gemini, Neptune 11 Aries,
Pluto 11 Aquarius, Chiron 13 Taurus

1.1.2032:
Jupiter 11 Capricorn, Saturn 18 Gemini,
Uranus 25 Gemini, Neptune 13 Aries,
Pluto 13 Aquarius, Chiron 17 Taurus

1.1.2033:
Jupiter 7 Aquarius, Saturn 4 Cancer,
Uranus 30 Gemini, Neptune 16 Aries,
Pluto 14 Aquarius, Chiron 22 Taurus

1.1.2034:
Jupiter 5 Pisces, Saturn 19 Cancer,
Uranus 4 Cancer, Neptune 18 Aries,
Pluto 16 Aquarius, Chiron 27 Taurus

1.1.2035:
Jupiter 6 Aries, Saturn 4 Leo,
Uranus 9 Cancer, Neptune 20 Aries,
Pluto 17 Aquarius, Chiron 3 Gemini

1.1.2036:
Jupiter 11 Taurus, Saturn 19 Leo,
Uranus 14 Cancer, Neptune 22 Aries,
Pluto 19 Aquarius, Chiron 9 Gemini

1.1.2037:
Jupiter 19 Gemini, Saturn 3 Virgo,
Uranus 18 Cancer, Neptune 25 Aries,
Pluto 20 Aquarius, Chiron 15 Gemini

1.1.2038:
Jupiter 27 Cancer, Saturn 17 Virgo,
Uranus 23 Cancer, Neptune 27 Aries,
Pluto 22 Aquarius, Chiron 23 Gemini

1.1.2039:
Jupiter 2 Virgo, Saturn 30 Virgo,
Uranus 28 Cancer, Neptune 29 Aries,
Pluto 23 Aquarius, Chiron 1 Cancer

1.1.2040:
Jupiter 2 Libra, Saturn 12 Libra,
Uranus 3 Leo, Neptune 1 Taurus,
Pluto 25 Aquarius, Chiron 10 Cancer

1.1.2041:
Jupiter 29 Libra, Saturn 24 Libra,
Uranus 8 Leo, Neptune 4 Taurus,
Pluto 26 Aquarius, Chiron 21 Cancer

1.1.2042:
Jupiter 25 Scorpio, Saturn 5 Scorpio,
Uranus 12 Leo, Neptune 6 Taurus,
Pluto 27 Aquarius, Chiron 3 Leo

1.1.2043:
Jupiter 19 Sagittarius, Saturn 16 Scorpio,
Uranus 17 Leo, Neptune 8 Taurus,
Pluto 29 Aquarius, Chiron 17 Leo

1.1.2044:
Jupiter 14 Capricorn, Saturn 27 Scorpio,
Uranus 22 Leo, Neptune 10 Taurus,
Pluto 30 Aquarius, Chiron 3 Virgo

1.1.2045:
Jupiter 11 Aquarius, Saturn 8 Sagittarius,
Uranus 27 Leo, Neptune 13 Taurus,
Pluto 1 Pisces, Chiron 20 Virgo

1.1.2046:
Jupiter 9 Pisces, Saturn 18 Sagittarius,
Uranus 2 Virgo, Neptune 15 Taurus,
Pluto 3 Pisces, Chiron 7 Libra

1.1.2047:
Jupiter 11 Aries, Saturn 28 Sagittarius,
Uranus 7 Virgo, Neptune 17 Taurus,
Pluto 4 Pisces, Chiron 24 Libra

1.1.2048:
Jupiter 16 Taurus, Saturn 8 Capricorn,
Uranus 12 Virgo, Neptune 20 Taurus,
Pluto 5 Pisces, Chiron 10 Scorpio

1.1.2049:
Jupiter 25 Gemini, Saturn 18 Capricorn,
Uranus 16 Virgo, Neptune 22 Taurus,
Pluto 7 Pisces, Chiron 24 Scorpio

1.1.2050:
Jupiter 2 Leo, Saturn 28 Capricorn,
Uranus 21 Virgo, Neptune 24 Taurus,
Pluto 8 Pisces, Chiron 3 Sagittarius

Pluto beyond 2050
February 24, 2068: into Aries
April 23, 2096: into Taurus
June 16, 2127: into Gemini
August 15, 2157: into Cancer
August 25, 2183: into Leo

Neptune beyond 2050
May 13, 2052: into Gemini
July 4, 2065: into Cancer
September 2, 2078: into Leo
September 5, 2092: into Virgo
November 22, 2105: into Libra
December 4, 2119: into Scorpio
December 20, 2130: into Sagittarius
January 5, 2148: into Capricorn
January 16, 2162: into Aquarius
March 20, 2175: into Pisces

Meaning of The Mathematics of Time

Advanced children and their grandchildren will grasp the mathematics of time outlined in these pages. They see its meaning via direct knowing. It is with these exceptional and gifted **seeing children** in mind, that this astrologer made his knowing available to mankind, when Jupiter aligned with Pluto in the Galactic Centre. And who is to say that some of us will not be returning here when Uranus aligns with Neptune in Aquarius – the sign it rules? Cosmic clock work mechanisms are easy to read when we focus our mind on the movements of beautiful simplicity.

Jupiter spends a year in each sign, magnifying its quality; whereas *Saturn* covers about twelve degrees per year and thus spends about two and a half years in a sign, bringing form and structure to issues governed by that sign. *Chiron* – planetoid ruling themes of healing, teaching and higher forms of magic – a most important point in every birth chart – takes an erratic orbit of fifty years around the Zodiac, so that an average per sign is not indicated. Aspects made between Chiron, Saturn, and Uranus are revealing because Chiron is seen as an inter-dimensional portal bridging established and untried concepts of knowing.

Chiron-Uranus-Neptune alignments are more impressive, as they gage the progress of *techno-spirituality*, and with it the knowing level of man. This book – **ForeSeen** – is its guided navigator. 2010 to 2012 see a long tandem passage of Chiron, ever so slowly approaching – and then passing – Neptune, in the last degrees of Aquarius, leading into Pisces, while Uranus leaves Pisces to move into Aries. If the fabled Mayan time line marker has any relevance at all, it is to be found in this most elusive of all alignments – symbolized by *The Finger of God –* or *Yod* aspect; 2013 and 2026 being the significant key zones.

Uranus, Neptune and Pluto – seen in symbiosis – show the transformational developments and collective state of mind the earth is in. Liberator and awakener *Uranus* moves at a rate of about four degrees per year, spending seven years in one sign. It advances by 2047 into Virgo where it opposes Pluto in Pisces in the same degree axis as in 4-5 BC. This mirrors the change of paradigm, following the long standing 2013-2017 Uranus-Pluto square of ninety degrees that signals the societal turning point. Uranus passes in line of Neptune in Aquarius on 17 January 2165 – suggestive of highly networked time travel applications from off-earth.

Neptune and Pluto move at differing but similar speeds of one and a half to two degrees per year; they give each sign a long lasting light frequency imprint. Neptune, ruling psychism or imagination, begins to move faster than Pluto, and changes its angle so as to be in sixty degrees to Pluto by 2032, while the angle grows larger (seventy-two degrees) by 2050. In 2009 Neptune is in a fifty-two degree angle to Pluto, which is rather doubtful as a generational outlook. This means we move from fear-based behaviour (52) towards a cooperative (60) and then peaceful (72) attitude over the coming decades, until Pluto spends thirty years n Gemini.

In 2137, Pluto in Gemini opposes Neptune in Sagittarius in the axis of the two most important fixed stars, Aldebaran, watcher in the East, known as bull's eye, and Antares, watcher in the West, known as heart of the Scorpion, respectively. This rarest of all oppositions – aspect of fullest openness, equivalent of **The Obsidian Mirror of Seeing** – is the guided and *living technology;* meaning *"To Seek the Light to its own Solution."* It augurs the breakthrough for mankind to join its space-based allies within one life time. This is what designer creation has foreseen; and I shall meet you there...

~ Michael St.Clair

```
                    2020
            2021         2022
        2023                 2024
    2025         2026         2027
        2028                 2029
            2030         2031
                    2032
```

"Those who know don't talk, and those who talk don't know. Truth is never flashy; fancy words are rarely true. You don't have to leave your room to grasp what's going on in the world; nor do you have to look out the window to appreciate the intricacy of Cosmos. The farther you roam, the less you see. True Masters of The Light don't roam around – they see; they know. They don't just look – they understand. They don't do anything – and yet The Work gets done."

~ The St.Clair Tao

Michael St.Clair &

The Master of The Light

With the successful publication of his internationally acclaimed **Zen of Stars** in 2006, astrologer and seer Michael St.Clair first shared his almost surreal interactions with *The Master of The Light*. Using his visionary skills, and speaking the language of star magic, he weaves a story of future contact unparalleled in its depth and content. Whether *St.Clair* is *The Master of The Light* is for you to find out, as you experience and share his vision.

ForeSeen – Beyond Time is an advanced *hyper-dimensional guidance* for the most fascinating times humanity will ever witness. St.Clair's new mind teaching reveals that the *living time travel technology* is the human mind.

This book alters reality with light-encoded words, looking at our world through the seer eyes of the leading master astrologer. In this book, St.Clair delivers a mind-altering and precision-guided prophecy. As part of the new mind, *ForeSeen* is designed for you to engineer the paths of your own incarnation from your own future. St.Clair – his master of the light, and his work – will change your life, as he frees mankind, one soul at a time.

St.Clair created *NewMind Technologies* – his international consulting group – via *First Contact*. He advises people to *seek safe places* and to *engineer islands of light* communities, where they will intelligently sail the seas of change. He advocates sustainable living, natural health and the use of orgone energy to rebalance the earth. The sane future is open source, hands on, innovations, created and shared by people developing networked solutions, using local resources. The power of our imagination will shift the global mind beyond the grey zone of commerce, and into an existence worth living. St.Clair speaks directly to the soul when he says: *"The human mind is the technology of the future."*

St.Clair's compelling documentary at *Château Chillon* – the masterful video shot by *Hollywood* producer director *Kerry Lynn Cassidy* – has been met with increasing awareness and praise. This stunning interview provoked significant interest across the internet, inspiring many to look beyond The Matrix.

The alliance between St.Clair and The Master of The Light is part of one of the oldest mythologies known to man. When you see your world through the eyes of tomorrow, you enter into a transformative relationship with your own time travelling awareness – the *Navigator Contact*.

In *ForeSeen* Michael St.Clair picks up where Stanley Kubrick's *2001 – A Space Odyssey* left off. Disclosure reveals human governments are not in control of planet earth. By 2050 these concepts will be understood by societies intent on achieving convergence with their innermost self. St.Clair shows how our future selves are the guidance of the future, communicating with mankind across the bridge of time. He reveals the 13th consciousness, beyond time, illuminating the mind of man and re-establishing the ancient science of the soul.

St.Clair gives essential astrological information about the core navigator codex, activated through conscious awareness, allowing the spirit to time travel the paths of its own existence. The spiritual sciences were lost as individuals forfeited their innate ability to understand the guidance of their own design. The Codex is embedded within the light encoded DNA, resonating to create the future. St.Clair connects the mysteries of Atlantis with the extra-terrestrial origins of humanity, and predicts that it is our destiny to return to the stars.

"Either we abandon the long-honored Theory of Relativity, or we cease to believe that we can engage in continued accurate prediction of the future. Indeed, knowing the future raises a host of questions which cannot be answered under conventional assumptions unless one first projects an Observer outside of Time and, second, nullifies all movement. If you accept the Theory of Relativity, it can be shown that Time and the Observer must stand still in relationship to each or inaccuracies will intervene. This would seem to say that it is impossible to engage in accurate prediction of the future. How, then, do we explain the continued seeking after this visionary goal by respected scientists?"

~ Frank Herbert, Children of Dune

"Wise people are not always educated; educated people are not necessarily smart, let alone intelligent. Good people never argue; people who argue are bad news. Knowing things makes one smart; knowing yourself makes you wise. To rule others, one must be powerful – to rule yourself, you must be strong. If I have only what I need, I have true wealth. If we never give up, we find a way. If you stay true to yourself, you will never be lost. If you stay aware your whole life, you will have truly lived – and made a difference."

~ The St.Clair Tao

Born in Switzerland on 28 February 1959, the renowned author and leading world councillor studied law and political sciences. He served as intelligence officer and aide-de-camp to a senior Swiss army general, and he advised high profile men in special situations. Today he guides people on issues pertaining to karmic vocation, teaching that life is all about timing. Working fluently in many languages, he counsels a growing international clientele, showing them how to extract themselves from the illusions of society, to live functional and healthy lives.

Among St.Clair's noted 1999 predictions were rising oil and gold prices, the falling dollar, collapse of housing markets, the 2000 ballot recount, as well as future elections and re-elections of key heads of states. He predicted global land degradation, wars and ever more powerful hurricanes, while developing his highly original insights about the future mind of mankind.

St.Clair – leading mundane astrologer – writes in-depth yearly personalized horoscopes, based on his clients or nations charts, using advanced seer astrology, steeped in Cosmic knowing. His intense work, a tool of The 13ᵗʰ Consciousness Activation, designed by his **NewMind Technologies** *consulting group, serves as guidance and cosmic positioning system. Consulted daily by thousands of surfers, his trendsetting websites are beacons of light shining out across the oceans of the Internet. Both feature his credited radio and video interviews. He runs an unusual and confidential global consulting practice, advising individuals and groups to enact meaningful solutions to fast approaching social change.*

Passage11.com – Zenofstars.org

Printed in the United States
102282LV00002B/164/A